SHIFTING SAND

Charles C Hadfield

2QT Limited (Publishing)

First Edition published 2017
2QT Limited (Publishing)
Settle, North Yorkshire BD24 9RH
www.2qt.co.uk

Cover deisgn Charlotte Mouncey
Images suppplied by iStockphoto.com

This is a work of fiction and any resemblance to any person, living or
dead, is purely coincidental. The place names mentioned maybe real but
have no connection with the events in this book.

Printed in Great Britain by Lightning Source UK Ltd

A CIP catalogue record for this book is available
from the British Library
ISBN 978-1-912014-85-9

To headaches and perseverance...

CONTENTS

Chapter 1

Happy Family

Ordinarily, life is a procession of missed buses and a succession of wrong turnings. The key to unlocking happiness and success lies in quickly identifying the numerous chances and opportunities which present themselves before manipulating them thoroughly and exploiting them ruthlessly. Obviously, a golden opportunity can prove extremely lucrative but it must be considered carefully and examined closely before decisively seizing the day, as he who hesitates is lost.

Previously, I had declined or disregarded offers to study economics at the nearby university, invest in a friend's flourishing landscape business and purchase a tranche of heavily discounted shares that were being sold off by the greedy government of the time. Undoubtedly, if I'd had a little more courage and foresight and taken advantage of any one of these, today I would be much wiser, more content and considerably wealthier. Unafraid to take a gamble with my capital – my natural instinct is to have a flutter – but in the past both the timing and decisions were wide of the mark. As a result, I promised myself that if another certainty came along, I would grab it with both hands. So, temptation was irresistible when the next money-making scheme materialised and rushed in like a fool, only to suffer devastating consequences.

My name is Mike Carpenter. Born during 1990, I was still living happily with my parents and elder brother in a three-bedroomed semi-detached house with lovingly maintained front and rear gardens in the outskirts of Sheffield. It is an area that I would struggle to describe as affluent or desirable. It is highly improbable that anyone from this socially and economically deprived district would feature in *Who's Who*; they are more likely to appear in *Who's That?* Under-referenced in the multitude of where-to-go guide books stocked by tourist information centres, Woodhouse cannot be compared to Las Vegas with its glitz, glamour and countless buried secrets; instead it is a dispirited place rather like Gomorrah. The surrounding community is low on hedonism but high on hardship; the one thing the hardy folk of this working-class enclave, who consider knives and forks to be jewellery, have in common is abject poverty.

Although it has a glorious industrial past, the city faces an uncertain future due in part to the demise of the coal industry and continuing overseas pressure on the steel sector. The gas lamps, hansom cabs and costermongers of yesteryear have vanished into the mists of time, replaced by energy-efficient lighting, fume-belching automobiles and grubby convenience stores. The evocative sounds of children playing in the park, hawkers shouting in the street and factory hooters signalling the first shift have been silenced by the redevelopment of recreational fields, red tape and redundant workplaces. The pleasant smells of home-baked bread, wood-fuelled fires and pipe tobacco have been smothered by the stench of fast-food takeaways, diesel emissions and weed smokers. The offices of bygone times, where filing cabinets clattered, typewriters chattered and personnel nattered, have been automated by computers, mobile phones and vending machines.

You get the picture.

In my opinion the young women of the borough are unattractive, uneducated and unfit, so when they go on a night out together, they look like a pack of swamp donkeys and behave like wild animals. With chests as flat as a rugby fifteen singing the national anthem, they have little appeal.

Once, while having a conversation in the pub with my last steady girlfriend, I asked her which was her favourite Bruegel.

'Cream cheese,' she answered. Then she amazed me still further by enquiring with genuine concern, and within a haze of putrid perfume, whether Jägerbombs were real weapons of mass destruction.

Contaminated by hate and diseased by distrust, Susan was lardy, pallid and very ripe. She was neither familiar with the robust language of diplomacy nor particularly tactful and she was certainly no slave to fashion. When she spoke, she sounded like her lips had been sewn together and were now slowly coming unstitched. She drank like a fish, ate like a horse and was grumpier than a bishop's cat. A cinema fanatic and a knowledgeable film geek, she possessed an awesome collection of vinyl and an enormous array of shoes. She was in her late twenties and still lived with her black-hearted and meddlesome mother, who was daft as a brush and stank of stale urine.

Prior to our parting of the ways, she piled on a lot of weight and took to wearing a kaftan which put me in mind of an unpegged tent. Her attitude towards me deteriorated to such an extent that all she ever said was, 'Fetch me this, bring me that, take away the other.'

Things came to a head and at one point I seriously toyed with the idea of murdering her and prayed for a dark night, isolated woodland and shallow grave. I abandoned the idea after she ditched me unexpectedly.

A few months later, I recognised her with a new boyfriend on an episode of the *Jeremy Kyle Show* entitled 'That Greedy Pig Ate My Benefit Cheque'. She was as fat as a whale. In retrospect, I can't recall any physical attraction, romantic spark or stimulating conversation throughout our most unsuitable partnership.

My parents are in their mid fifties, still very active and totally devoted not only to each other but also to their two sons. Mr and Mrs Carpenter had moved from Altrincham following their wedding and had just celebrated their pearl anniversary. They had been childhood sweethearts since junior school; the unbroken courtship continued through college and they eventually tied the knot in 1984 at their quaint, local rural church which, according to gossip, had a window designed by Burne-Jones.

They lauded and applauded their children, as well as offering a safe haven in a turbulent world. These were no doubt significant factors in why, apart from the usual youthful indiscretions, our lives were largely stable and untroubled. However, I found their friends intensely boring, irritating and very '*Daily Telegraph*', particularly the scrotum-shrivelling dullards, the Browns. They lived down the road but frequently came round in the evenings for a cup of tea, slice of seed cake and less-than riveting conversation.

Capable of felling you with a look and lifting with a word, my mother Mary is firm but fair. She is delicately built and possesses an effortless energy. She is of average height, with hair that is turning white and a sunshine smile. Employed as a receptionist at a busy dental surgery, she is legendary for her dynamism and organisational skills, which are often abused by the assortment of clubs and societies to which she belongs. Blessed with a cheerful and gentle disposition, she radiates an old-fashioned decency and warmth. She is also exceedingly efficient, extremely lively and most popular; she is certainly not a shuffling, crotchety old lady.

To us, my mum is an angel on earth, the lynchpin of our unit and deeply loved by all. She is very house-proud, a keen gardener and a stickler for tradition. Every Sunday, without fail, she attends morning worship, cooks a roast dinner and prepares high tea, of which a pink blancmange, fruit jelly or strawberry trifle is the highlight.

By contrast, my father is a more circumspect man; he takes a more measured and level-headed approach to problems. Bernard is over six feet tall, thickset and with boxer's shoulders. He stands no nonsense, is down-to-earth and does not suffer fools gladly. As tough as teak, brave as a bulldog and tenacious as a lobster, he has worked for the last twelve years as a typesetter at a well-established printers, where the pay is modest and the hours long.

My dad has always looked out for me, from searching for monsters under the bed at night when I was a youngster to telling me that psycho Sue was a loser when she dumped me just before my nineteenth birthday. When I was a child he taught me to ride a bike, took me carp fishing and showed me how to fly a kite as well as helping with homework, building me a tree house and instructing me in tying a Windsor knot. He is extremely supportive, infinitely patient and has always encouraged me to give anything a go. In a world where the word 'greatest' is always overused he was – and still is – my hero.

Occasionally, while engaging in the many and varied discussions we had when I was growing up, my dad would reminisce and expatiate on more easy-going and liberal times. His unshakeable belief that things were better in his day was enhanced by his recollection that everything was rocking, groovy and the Beatles were in their pomp, McCartney got mobbed everywhere, Che Guevara rode a camel on the beach and Dizzy Gillespie played with a snake charmer. Dad claimed that, as a youth, he wore Teddy boy suits and raced his motorbike at the seaside. Everybody was into free love. When old people refer to the golden age, the glory days, happier times, it is the casual, promiscuous and swinging sixties that they are talking about, which probably denotes how bad things are at the present. It is never a case of 'remember the great time we had last week'; no, it is 'the fantastic times we enjoyed in '63'. That was fun, as the nightingales of the decade sang; women bathed in bikinis and a pound was worth something. It was an era when England won the World Cup, Bob Beamon broke the world record for the long jump at the Mexico Olympics and Arkle reigned supreme. Dad frequented Wimpy Bars and strutted his stuff at dance halls. Double Diamond worked wonders, sherbet dips were dabbed, Black Jacks chewed and gobstoppers sucked as *Paint Your Wagon* rolled into town, *Kes* flew away and Cathy came home.

Although it is arguable that all of these things belong to that ageing generation, he was, as I kept reminding him, only born in 1960. It is doubtful, therefore, that he witnessed at first hand the events he described, wore the fashions or took part in any of the activities. It is probable that he simply watched them on a shadowy television, read about them in an inky newspaper or listened to them on a crackly wireless.

Nowadays he chooses to languish in his favourite armchair, having finally accepted his increasing age with an equanimity honed by a lifetime of experience as he tackles the crossword, crunches Rich Tea biscuits and listens to Radio Two. He thinks that *Wake Up To Wogan* is wonderful and *Sing Something Simple* is sensational. The rock-and-roll years are now just a fading memory as the records by the Stones, The Who and Dylan are stored in the loft of destiny, the news of heart transplants, men walking on the moon and Kennedy's assassination are confined to the memory bank of time, while the fashionable kipper ties, winkle-pickers and flowery shirts are discarded to the dustbin of history. Sometimes, though, I was forced to jog his memory that Elvis is dead, Lennon was shot and even Georgie Best has gone to a better place.

Throughout our formative years, my brother Kieran and I fought like cat and dog, mainly due to my superior academic ability. I was more than capable of out-thinking, outwitting and out-writing him as he did not retain the sense he was born with. But as we moved through adolescence our bond strengthened and we became best mates.

Physically, Kieran developed into an imposing character with a jutting jaw and bulging biceps and he became notorious and feared in the immediate neighbourhood. Although not especially articulate and noisier than a battalion of soldiers enjoying themselves in a brothel, he had a fondness for heavy drinking and off-colour jokes. Nevertheless, he saved my bacon on more than one occasion by forcefully recovering my cash from a swindling second-hand car dealer and warning me off luscious Linda. With hair the colour of corn, rapacious eyes and twice my age, I was nearly 'Chatterleyed' when labouring casually in her garden, as I fiddled in her foliage, trimmed her bush and forked her damp patch, while her brutal husband, instead of working away in Dubai, was about to be released after serving a four-year sentence for actual bodily harm.

When he was a teenager, Kieran spent a lot of time crying and playing with himself in his room instead of reading and revising for his exams. In the rough school where pupils left with ASBOs, staff brought extra dinner money and the Ofsted inspector carried a flick knife, Kieran's final report alluded to this dereliction of duty by mentioning that he was lazy and needed to buckle down more, before adding, 'he does try – but not very much and not too often.' The headmaster stated, rather prophetically, that Kieran was the student most likely to lie about everything, rig a raffle or betray his nearest and dearest for self-gratification.

While he was still a kid and extremely accident-prone, I remember Kieran somehow managed to cut himself on a pair of safety scissors before getting his double up by splitting open his head on the rounded edge of a coffee table. He caused mayhem wherever he went; his cavalier attitude towards women carried him by the seat of his pants and continues to do so to this day. His concept of foreplay is to kick the empty beer cans off the unmade bed and his notion of safe sex means not telling the girl where he lives. He thinks that love is a score in tennis. He had scant regard for life's finer things and even less appreciation of its rules.

***

It is shameful to say that, as a Yorkshire man, I hate cricket; it probably means that I am a traitor. When I was little, I was not the fine specimen of masculinity that I am now; I was skinny and uncoordinated so I never got picked for any team games or sports. While all my friends were enjoying themselves, I was forced to sit and watch from the sidelines, even when they were playing in my garden with my bat and ball.

I eventually switched my focus to boxing but even that was no picnic. The sergeant major of a trainer forced me to run until my feet were like raw lumps of liver; I pumped iron until every sinew in my body begged for mercy and pummelled the punchbag until my fists were as hard as jackhammers. Needless to say, following a challenging short period in which the other fighters nicknamed me 'the washing line', I threw in the towel and turned to an alternative hobby.

Aged eleven, I persevered at the piano for eighteen tedious, talentless and tuneless months as my miserable music master, Mr Maxwell, moodily moaned and groaned in disbelief while I plinked and plonked my way clumsily through 'Chopsticks'. The aspirations I harboured of one day becoming an overpaid concert pianist were dashed after a truly frustrating lesson, during which I persisted in demonstrating no progress. Mr Maxwell, having reached the end of his tether and in absolute despair, ended it all. Following his poorly attended funeral, my mother explained that he was subject to severe depression and deeply troubled; she insisted that I should not blame myself for him resorting to the rope. It was not my inability to graduate from the basic level that removed his will to live.

With my placid disposition, I am generally the type of person who revels in routine and enjoys inertia; I am all in favour of progress, as long as it does not bring about change. Lacking a high degree of personal ambition and achievable dreams, I much prefer to maintain the status quo or just plod along. I am not a fan of upheaval and change but, as somebody once told me, as a fledgling adult you can silently endure, break down or learn to fight back. However, sometimes you cannot keep putting gratification on hold; you need to stand up, pack up and explore the labyrinth of life or it will pass you by.

Not since the 1461 disagreement between the Houses of York and Lancaster was so much shock and consternation expressed than that shown by my friends and family when, without warning and with a tinge of self-doubt, I announced that I was about to set out on my voyage of discovery. So, with my passport in order, inoculations completed and armed with a pocket phrasebook, I prepared to cross the border to try my luck, seek my fortune and find my metier among the bright lights and fleshpots of Manchester.

CHAPTER 2

Flying the Nest

The welcoming sound of a boiling kettle and the mouth-watering aroma of breakfast being prepared downstairs jolted me from a deep and reviving sleep on that final Saturday in July 2010. Through a small gap in the curtains, I could see that a giant sun like a Jaffa orange had appeared. The 'chacker' alarm of a blackbird became audible as I started to wrestle with the myriad of thoughts swirling in my mind. This was moving day, a fresh start, the beginning of a new chapter in my life. On the one hand I felt the excitement and anticipation of a young shaver aged just twenty, striking out into the big wide world alone; on the other, I was worried about leaving behind the comfort and security of my friends and relatives in order to discover who knew what.

With these mixed emotions uppermost, I dressed hurriedly and descended hungrily to the kitchen. I was pleasantly surprised to see my mother cooking a traditional fry-up. This was a rare spectacle; the last time the Carpenters had sat down together for a 'full monty' was some four years previously on my father's forty-sixth birthday. Since then my mother had made it plain that the males of the household were old enough to fend for themselves.

With tremendous relish we tucked into the crispy bacon, overcooked sausages, dippy egg, sliced mushrooms, chopped tomatoes and fried slice; if our local GP had witnessed us demolishing all this cholesterol-raising food, he would have doubtless suffered a heart attack of his own. After polishing off the 'belly-buster', my brother reminded me that the removal team was due at one o'clock, as confirmed during yesterday's visit to the pub.

My recollection of the previous evening was somewhat hazy. Kieran had frogmarched me to the Wise Owl for a farewell drink or two with the lads. Although the bar was situated less than half a mile from our house, it was not the nearest; we affectionately referred to it as our local because it was the only one in the vicinity that had not yet imposed a lifetime ban on my elder brother. The venue, despite its lack of charm or redeeming features, magnetically attracted an eclectic mixture of customers from the surrounding impoverished council estates. On Fridays in particular, the jumble-sale-clad misfits would shoehorn in and put the beer away as though their necks were on fire in an effort to not only drown the stresses and strains of the working week but also temporarily escape from their humdrum domestic lives.

When we arrived, the taproom was heaving with the usual assortment of builders, plumbers and labourers, all thirstily seeking salvation in the bottom of a glass. The majority of the clientele were male, some single, others married and the remainder still undecided which way to turn. The general tone of the conversation was earthy and punctured by obscenities, and focused primarily on football, beer and females. Political correctness, equal opportunities and women's lib had no place in there; bigotry, discrimination and being judgmental ruled supreme.

It was not an environment to take a young lady for a convivial, quiet and trouble-free date; in fact, it was the kind of tight-knit community where everyone knew you, your business and your secrets. This was demonstrated by the regulars acknowledging and speaking to Kieran, while eyeing me with distrust and suspicion. I suppose that was to be expected given that I was not a regular visitor, whereas he was. Wearing a Sheffield Wednesday shirt while holding court with his cronies, he was in his element.

We had just finished our fifth pint when the relocation specialists unceremoniously entered the vibrant bar. The Bonser Brothers had been hired and paid the previous week and were scheduled to transfer my goods and chattels to a brave new world the following day. Barry was the smaller of the two men, with cauliflower ears, straggly hair and a face at which you could take offence. Although physically powerful, he was stupid; thanks to the use of steroids, his upper body was so well developed that, when he walked, he resembled a cube on legs.

His brother Paul was over six feet six tall, built like a barn and had nothing but straw in his loft. His face was covered by a large beard which came down further on one side than the other and a moustache which was sinisterly dark and rectangular. He was also extremely muscular and displayed a tattoo on his hairy right forearm which depicted two crossed knives and a slogan: 'These blades are United'. This indolent but much revered pair of powerhouses were so dissimilar in appearance that the crazy and clueless in the spit-and-sawdust pubs they frequented constantly questioned their parentage.

Paul spotted me skulking in the corner next to a glum-eyed, one-armed bandit. He strode like a colossus across the sticky floor, the ay-uppers, ecky-thumpers and ee-by-gummers scattering like confetti in his wake. He sat down heavily on a low, creaking bar stool and rasped in a voice which sounded like it had been raised on barbed wire and broken beer bottles, 'Nah then, sithee. All set for tomorrer?'

'Yes,' I replied timidly. 'There isn't much to move, just a few boxes, a couple of cases, a bed, sofa, fridge, that sort of thing.'

'That sounds alreet. Champion. Not too bad,' he remarked before downing most of his drink in a single gulp. 'We'll have you shifted in a jiffy.' He crashed his huge fist loudly onto the table before getting to his feet. Then, leaning forward and silently burping a vile combination of alcohol and cigarette fumes directly into my face while winking knowingly, he asked, 'Hast given us the two-er for the job?'

'Yes, I gave it to you last weekend when I saw you in here and treated you to a lager to seal the deal,' I retorted rather indignantly.

'Oh yeah,' he said, smiling into his beard and tapping the side of his head. 'I was just testing thee. I'll sithee tomorrer and don't forget.'

'What?' I interrupted.

'Where tha loyalties lie. Tha roots and the Yorkshire motto of hear all, see all and say nowt, eat all, sup all and pay nowt. And if tha ever does owt for nowt, do it for thissen.' He cackled before playfully punching my shoulder and striding away while I winced with pain and blasphemed inwardly.

Prior to lunch on the red-letter day of my move, where a sweltering sun was already burning down fiercely and the weather appeared set for another perfect summer's afternoon, I spent a little time ensuring that everything was packed, boxed and bagged. Then my mum meticulously double-checked my work. Usually at the weekend, she was outside in the garden, lovingly tending her flowers, shrubs and bushes or food shopping at the crowded and chaotic supermarket. Today was different, however; as time ticked by, she grew increasingly anxious. In an attempt to keep busy, she dusted, vacuumed and arranged the cushions on the sofa before rearranging them and offering to make yet another cup of tea.

My father seemed calmer and more relaxed. Still in his slippers, he reclined in his generously stuffed armchair and deliberated over the crossword. Lifting his head, peering over the top of his newspaper at me and pretending to struggle with a clue, he mischievously challenged, 'Five down, three across, four letters, ending in IT. Found at the bottom of a budgie's cage.'

I wished that I had been given a pound for every time he tried that tiresome joke. I pretended to think before answering with bored indifference, 'Grit.'

After a short while, and having reached the climax of his mental masturbation, he folded the paper neatly, placed it on the coffee table and ruffled idly through the periodicals before saying chillingly, 'This time tomorrow, Mike, you'll be in your own place, all alone and having to fend for yourself.'

I had often made the comparatively short journey to Manchester, primarily to watch United play at the theatre of dreams, but latterly it was in search of work and accommodation. Earlier in the month I'd attended a series of job interviews and secured a permanent position as a sales executive within a friendly, family-run, double glazing firm in the Northern Quarter. In addition, I looked at several properties; unfortunately they were all in various states of disrepair and neglect. Eventually, though, I found a one-bedroom apartment on the east side of the city which was, as the estate agent described, within easy access of the motorway network, close to an airport and near to excellent bus and rail links. Although the monthly rent on the mildewed residence was just about manageable, the initial deposit was prohibitive but, with the generous financial assistance from the Bank of Mum and Dad, I raised the necessary funds.

Both the cash-in-handers arrived promptly. With our willing help, Sheffield's answer to the Chuckle Brothers had the dented, scuffed, lopsided Luton fully loaded within an hour.

At this point, the significance of the moment tightened its grip on my emotions. Crunching up the gravel path to the front door, where the mahonias nodded stiffly at me, the berberis arched its branches like a fawning cat and the cereus stretched out its arms and curtsied to the breeze, I thought that I would miss them all. Lifting my gaze, I saw my mother standing sad-faced on the threshold. She was on the verge of crying as the realisation finally dawned that her youngest son was leaving home and going to live in the morally corrupt metropolis.

We embraced tenderly before holding each other tightly for several moments, neither of us wishing to let go. She began to weep softly. Through her breathless sobs she blurted, 'Your room will always be here for you, son. Come back whenever you want. Bring your dirty washing and come for your tea. If you don't settle in, your dad will bring you back. We will always be here. Never forget that this is where you live.'

When we disentangled ourselves, I tried to comfort her. 'I'll keep in touch. It's only a forty-minute drive, it's not the other side of the world.' Then I added, 'I'll give you a ring when I've arrived and unpacked.'

I turned, biting my lip and thinking what a gorgeous day as the sun shone, the birds sang, the bees were sated with honey. I was setting out on an exciting adventure. I retraced my steps to the gently purring car where my father and brother sat gloomily looking the other way. I didn't dare look over my shoulder at the figure framed in the doorway, dabbing her eyes; the sight of her would surely have turned my trickle of tears to a torrent.

Making our way from the suburbs and meandering through the quaint, picturesque hamlets of South Yorkshire, we followed the daffodil-coloured van as it swayed like a pendulum and rode the contours, humps and hollows of the uneven and winding road. Breaking the lengthy silence which had prevailed since our departure, my dad fanned himself with a clean handkerchief. He pointed accusingly at the van and stated bluntly, 'Bloody hell, we've got to come back in that when we've dropped you off and one of those clowns will be driving.'

Engrossed in our own thoughts, neither of us responded. The sun, now past its zenith, refused to surrender its intensity. Lowering the window as we ascended the spine of Britain, I smelt the lovely scents of freshly cut grass and recently trimmed hedges which, fused with the waft of soil naturally dried by the elements and the fragrance of wild flowers, created a uniquely British potpourri. On the hillside to the right was a low white farm building with a red tiled roof; a straw scarecrow was slumped at the gate and tied by a piece of bleached string. Beyond, a flock of sullen sheep wandered aimlessly in an unfenced field and on the horizon a group of ramblers tramped contentedly through the parched gorse and bracken with tattered rucksacks slung about their shoulders. To the left, a slope slipped sharply to a shallow stream, which was straddled by a narrow wooden bridge. I watched a merlin scything purposefully through the clear azure skies above the gaunt crags of picture-postcard England.

After a while an unmarked police car flagged us down and a ferocious-looking female officer enquired as to whether we had spotted any members of the travelling community acting suspiciously during our journey. Noting our mystified and negative response, she inspected my licence before waving us on. At the brow of the hill where the road squeezed round a barren outcrop of gritstone, we passed an isolated thatched old inn with a spacious beer garden full of thirsty drinkers taking advantage of the fresh air and unrelenting sunshine. A gypsy caravan was parked in the shade with a piebald horse who nodded his head somnolently and flicked his tail at the bothersome flies. The panoramic view made it possible to see for miles and Kieran fantasised that he could make out the donkeys plodding wearily up and down Blackpool Beach, hear the waves breaking against the shore and even taste the salty spray of the sea.

Starting the descent to our final destination, however, the landscape changed as the natural beauty and untamed wildness of the trans-Pennine route gave way to a concrete urban sprawl. The imposing tower blocks, small red-brick houses and gloomy monstrous factories, where thin dribbles of blue smoke puttered aimlessly from the tall chimneys, revealed that we were now somewhere quite different. The scruffily dressed urchins played, oblivious to any dangers in the dirty and mean streets as they roamed among the scavenging dogs and mangy cats. This typically northern scene was reminiscent of paintings by L S Lowry, I thought, as we threaded our way through a warren of nameless, potholed streets until, quite by chance, we stumbled on our target.

The Bonsers climbed down from the wheezing, clapped-out vehicle which, by now, was in need of a good sluicing down with a hosepipe. They stretched lazily and lit up their fags before ambling cockily to the rear and starting to unload. I ascended a flight of stone stairs warily, paused momentarily and unlocked the door of the first-floor apartment. A musty, closed-up smell assaulted me.

Stark and bereft of colour, my new home was not a magnificent seat of English aristocracy with oak panelling, marble staircase and fine antiques; it was an unfurnished, one-bedroom bachelor pad, completely empty except for a single picture left hanging by a previous tenant. The paint was peeling, the radiators rattled and the floor was filthy. I kicked aside a pile of unopened post, unwanted leaflets and unread copies of *The Bugle* before warmly ushering in my helpers.

'It's not very big,' lamented Barry in a rough, tough voice, while chewing on a strawberry wine gum and sweating like a blacksmith.

'Well, there's only me,' I responded defensively. 'It shouldn't take you too long to bring everything in and get the place shipshape.'

Barry nodded in agreement and retreated outside with his partner as my father went into each room and flung open the windows to let the stale air out and new hope circulate.

The unloading process was completed speedily and, despite some minor bumping and scraping, the meagre amount of furniture was distributed appropriately before I handed Paul a crisp twenty and insisted that he bought a drink when they returned to the Owl. Kieran impatiently high-fived me, wished me all the best and trotted down the steps behind the others. My dad lingered for some time before he unexpectedly clasped my hand, inched forward and slipped his arm around my shoulders before affectionately kissing the top of my head. This bear of a man, who was not normally tactile, then enveloped me in his tree-trunk arms, hugged me firmly and whispered, 'Good luck, son. I'll miss you. Have you got everything you want? Do you need any more brass? We'll keep your room the same and I'll come to the rescue if you don't settle down. Just give me a call.'

'It'll be fine. Don't worry, I'll cope,' I interjected as my eyes moistened and a lump swelled in my throat.

He continued to hold me for a few tender seconds until he relinquished me and reversed to the exit. 'I'm proud of you, really proud,' he said as a parting shot and quietly left. Never in my memory had I witnessed or experienced such a show of emotion and affection from this man who ordinarily kept his feelings firmly under control. This godlike character, whom I considered indestructible and beyond reproach, was not given to such displays of sensitivity or acts of touchy-feeliness.

Rushing to the open window, I was just in time to catch a glimpse as he strode to the waiting vehicle with its engine running. He wiped his sleeve across his eyes and jumped aboard before the battered transporter lurched off, honked its horn, swung around the corner and disappeared from view.

I remained standing there, deep in thought for some time, trying to take stock of the toing and froing of the last few hours. I recalled reading in a book: '*People are like plants, they need their roots. If they are transported it can be very traumatic.*' Bearing this in mind, I repaired to the sagging sofa and flopped down, feeling isolated and desperate. I quickly spiralled into morose melancholy as an outpouring of homesickness began to manifest itself. Tears rolled down my cheeks before the floodgates opened fully and the grief gathered apace. Slumping to my knees, I prostrated myself on the disgusting carpet. Unable to staunch the sobs, I pounded the floor in frustration and bellowed, 'I want to go home, I want to go home,' as the unpacked cases gloated, the unopened boxes mocked and the untied bin liners sneered.

Sometime later, after the hurt had eased marginally, I resumed my stance at the window. I placed my fingers warily on the unclean sill and listened to the noises of an unfamiliar city. A mistle thrush hurled its song from the top of a sycamore at the end of my neighbour's garden and a motorbike roared throatily somewhere in the distance. On the pavement across the road, I observed a teenage mother gasping greedily at a roll-up as she wheeled her baby in a silver pram; trailing behind her was a stooped and wizened old man, shuffling unsteadily alongside his brown and white spotted spaniel. Further back, a blonde-haired little girl tried desperately to steer her pink tricycle in a straight line without using any hands. Glancing up, I surveyed a mackerel sky that portended the climatic conditions for Sunday. With my world in turmoil, I scanned the heavens for answers as a delicious smell of curry from a nearby takeaway drifted in on a light breeze.

The renewed enthusiasm to man up was short-lived. Returning to the three-seater, and in an effort to allay my mother's concerns, I telephoned and lied about my well-being before, unable to suppress the tears, I descended once more into abject misery. Evening deepened in the avenue and a cracked mirror, hanging loosely on the opposite wall, reflected the gloominess of my features.

CHAPTER 3

First Impressions

Four years later, and on the second Saturday in September, I basked in pleasurable dreams. With no discernible plans, I allowed myself the luxury of an extra half-hour in bed before catapulting out, going into the kitchen and, in an effort to maintain a reasonable standard of internal health, devoured a man-sized bowl of muesli washed down with a glass of fresh fruit juice.

The unscheduled lie-in had slightly delayed my weekend routine of visiting the local leisure centre and subjecting myself to a period of sustained physical punishment as a penance for the recent reckless alcohol, carbohydrate and saturated-fat intake. After washing and dressing, I put on my shoes and peered through the east-facing bedroom window. It was just possible to make out the distant outline of the hills where, according to an old Manchester saying: *'If you can't see the Pennines it's raining, but if you can it's about to start.'* With the gloom-sodden prospect of another wet day uppermost in my mind, I pulled on a waterproof jacket, grabbed my sports bag and scuttled outside to the car.

As usual at the weekend, the health club was crammed with energetic exercisers making full use of the many state-of-the-art facilities as they relentlessly strove for that elusive feel-good factor. After tiptoeing past a sleepy official, bypassing the arcade of vending machines and barging into the swarming changing room, I noticed the suffocating smell of antiperspirant and liniment; it overpowered the thick stench from a blocked toilet. The luminous Lycra-clad enthusiasts with their flashing designer trainers were warming up vigorously.

Instead of choosing the crowded badminton hall, occupied squash courts or packed swimming pool, I decided to start in the gym. Even in there, the static bikes, treadmills and rowing equipment were in full use so I was forced to start my regime on the heavy-looking weights. After adjusting the apparatus to an easier setting, I began the various pulling, pushing and pumping motions scientifically designed to hone and tone the physique in a fanciful attempt to achieve parity with the muscle-bound beefcakes who stretched and strained on either side.

Thirty exhausting minutes later, I switched my attention to the relative calmness of a high-tech stationary bicycle where, for a similar length of time, I pedalled gently with the aim of increasing my cardiovascular fitness while watching the wall-mounted monitors, which provided a much needed distraction from my thumping chest, stinging thighs and tight calves. Finally, it was time for the sophisticated running machine. Dropping the speed and incline to junior level, I stared stoically ahead while pounding breathlessly for five miles. At the conclusion of my masochistic visit I showered hurriedly and dragged myself out into the steady rain. I scanned the slate sky, which looked set in for the remainder of the day, before collapsing with fatigue into my vehicle and promised myself 'never again'.

Before lunch, I walked like C-3PO during an oil shortage into the warmth and dryness of the dimly lit betting shop. Life had changed a lot since my departure from Sheffield, I mused, while surveying the chapel of chance where the punters prayed to the Almighty for divine intervention in picking a winning Yankee or Canadian. I surveyed the speculators scrutinising the screens as they dabbled on the dogs and punted on the ponies. A nervous-looking gambler fretted in the corner, fidgeting and shifting his weight as he peeped at a horse race from Dubai through his fingers. His face reddened with excitement as the heavily backed favourite scrambled home by a nose.

My weekly ritual of placing an accumulator had continued unabated for some time, during which Lady Luck had remained a stranger. Two small returns are modest by anyone's standards. I suppose the reasons I persevered with this unrewarding folly of donating my hard-earned money to those needy and greedy bookmakers were firstly in the hope that one day I might hit the jackpot, and secondly it provided a discussion point – if not a source of amusement – among my friends They all seemed much more successful with their own selections.

On this never-to-be-forgotten morning, however, in a shop where more employees were taking the bets than paying out, I was about to beat the odds and my life would change forever.

I noticed that the regular members of staff were absent from behind the counter; they had been replaced by a pair of what I assumed to be new starters. Marjorie was in her forties, as big as a barrage balloon and with glasses so thick they must have been difficult to see through. She spoke with a refined Edinburgh accent, looked like an evil, mischievous sprite and, as I found out later, was married to a bankrupt garage proprietor with a foul temper and a taste for whisky. She seemed to be on edge, indifferent and abrupt, an attitude that I reckoned might have been improved by some further customer service training.

In contrast, her colleague was in her mid twenties, slimly built and with shiny mahogany hair, shot by copper highlights and cut short to emphasise her slender neck. Her unfurrowed white brow, broad smile and smooth, unblemished throat marked her out as she sat calmly at her position in a cerise, company-issued blouse and black skirt. A green plastic name tag perched on her pouting right breast simply heralded 'Sandy'.

Avoiding the sombre, deep-voiced and continually coughing boggart, I chose the more appealing prospect. Shuffling across the grey-tiled floor, I hovered behind a bedraggled old woman who appeared alarmingly drunk for the time of day. She was clad in a shabby wet overcoat; she dug frantically into her purse before spraying a handful of loose change noisily on the ground. Quickly reverting to my Boy Scout training, I performed my good deed for the day by stooping stiffly to collect the coins and returning them to the flustered pensioner. Having declined her slurred insistence to take fifty pence for my trouble, I passed my completed slip under the protective shield and greeted the pretty brunette. 'Hello, how are you?' I asked coyly.

'Hi there. I'm fine, thank you,' she responded, with a degree of bashfulness and a quizzical look.

'I've not seen you in here before. Is it your first day?' I asked genially.

'Yes, I've just started with the company,' she confided. She scanned my slip and handed me a receipt together with the change from a ten-pound note.

I thanked her and stepped away from the counter. With a tinge of envy I watched a turbanned Asian gentleman collect a huge stack of twenties and, without counting them, stuffed them deep into his pocket. How liberating it would be to have sufficient funds to buy a new car or book a foreign holiday, I mused. Then a bead of sweat trickled down the nape of my neck when I spotted an unmistakable figure loitering near the gents.

By reputation, Biffo was unreliable, untrustworthy and should be avoided at all costs. Over six foot tall, with wild hair and a bloated face, he worked occasionally as an odd-job man for some very unsavoury characters and profited handsomely from their nefarious activities. Well-nourished and invariably overwatered, he could be found regularly in the various bars and pubs in the borough.

Slumped disconsolately against a narrow wooden shelf, above which a copy of the trade paper was pinned to the wall, Biffo was dressed in a long-sleeved shirt, buttoned to the wrists, and loose white trousers; he looked like the captain of the local cricket team. Despite his passion for, and an encyclopaedic knowledge of, greyhound racing, he looked like he had just suffered a number of financial reverses and was gloomier than a grave digger without a shovel.

'How is your luck? Have you had any winners?' I asked, tongue in cheek.

'Terrible,' he retorted. 'I've had more seconds than a ticking clock. Things are desperate. I'm badly off form and I've just lost this week's rent. My mother will go ballistic so I need an idea to recoup the cash. Have you got anything up your sleeve?' He cracked his knuckles in frustration.

I smiled wryly, keeping my thoughts to myself and, undeterred by his downbeat response, I changed the subject. 'Who's the new girl behind the glass?' I asked gesturing towards the stunner and keen to find out more.

He cast a cursory glance at her and said, 'I'm not sure, man. Word on the street is that she's some kind of a student. It's her first day, innit? But I wouldn't mind having a go, would you?' he asked sleazily. He perked up a little and dug an elbow into my ribs in an effort to garner support.

'You bet,' I replied blithely. I left him and shambled towards the door of the almost empty shop before peeking back and waving to Sandy. To my immense surprise, she tilted her head, raised a ringless left hand and gave me an amiable smile.

Outside in the fine drizzle, I began to consider that rarely, if ever, in my lifetime had I glimpsed a woman who ignited such an overwhelming instant attraction. Not only had she sown a seed in my mind but she'd also awoken a stirring in my loins, a sensation which had been dormant for longer than I cared to remember. With her swimming-pool-blue eyes, cute nose and luscious lips, she looked truly angelic; although others in the past had made a similar impression, it was certainly not at this level. There was something strikingly different this time. I have never believed in love at first sight, preferring to take the more measured approach of investing time and effort in getting to know and understand someone.

Hobbling along the pavement, trying to dodge the spray thrown up by a bronze hatchback which deliberately drove too close to the kerb, I slalomed in and out of the bustling shoppers. I was fleetingly tempted by the aroma wafting from Claire's coffee shop and the sight of people sipping lattes and eating home-made brandy snaps, served by a youth who did not look a day over thirteen, but I managed to resist. I rushed past the adjacent family butcher who carved, chopped and jointed Sunday's dinner before I browsed briefly in the second-hand book shop.

Across the road and adjoined to a gluten-free vegetarian restaurant called Take My Pulse, Mr Patel's minimart was busy when I went in to buy a pint of milk and a loaf of bread. I forced my way through the thronging, morbidly obese peasants, who choked the clean and antiseptic aisles. The junk-filled masses bulged shamelessly out of their knocked-off chavvy clothes, totally engrossed in scrimmaging around the selection of cheap strong booze and the multitude of buy one, get one free offers on chocolate and crisps. The queue to pay for my less than five items was slow-moving, however, due in part to an unfamiliar assistant with a villainous face and squint arguing with a customer about a refund on an already half-drunk bottle of Chilean Merlot. The problem was compounded by the seemingly insatiable appetite of the general public for lotto and scratch cards. These skill-less and addictive games, which rely entirely on fortune, were only devised to entice the plebs to part with their cash in the forlorn hope of striking it rich and thus being able to escape from their hitherto unfulfilled, worthless lives.

Hungry and thirsty, I returned to my bachelor pad and made myself a sandwich and a drink before sitting down in front of the television and flicking through the channels. Some time ago, I had given up on the national broadcaster, mainly because I felt it was failing in its mission statement of informing, educating and entertaining. Consequently I chose to subscribe to satellite TV where, in my opinion, the vast array of channels provided better value for money, especially where live sport and new films were concerned.

Chilling out on the sofa as the constantly changing football scores scrawled across the screen, my thoughts drifted to the dark-haired, good-looking girl I'd seen earlier. I wondered who she was, where she had come from. What was she about? Was this a gilt-edged opportunity, my big chance or just another Caramac wrapper of hope discarded on the dung heap of despair? My interest had been kindled and imagination captured and, despite my hitherto sceptical view that love is a box probably best left unopened, I now hoped the fickle finger of fate was at last pointing directly at my heart.

Some time had elapsed since my last physical encounter and I was more than ready to dip my toe into the often turbulent and sometimes murky waters of romance. Following my move from Sheffield I had only dated a handful of women but, for one reason or another, they were casual dalliances that soon petered out.

Within the first week of my tenancy, however, a female neighbour had introduced herself. Kylie was a twenty-one-year-old single mother with a three-year-old son and a fondness for bottled German lager. She was petite, heavy-eyed and as pale as Dutch cheese. When she spoke though, her uncultured southern accent grated as she persisted in dropping her aitches, mispronouncing words and insisted on calling everyone 'darling'. Furthermore, her disgusting habit of smoking was a real turnoff and the rasping cough and machine-gun-like laughter were extremely annoying. The child's unemployed father had absconded after failing to fulfil his promise of giving his partner the world, and just before the heavies called to collect an outstanding gambling debt. Kylie worked as and when she could for a secretarial agency but I suspect that even this role stretched her capabilities to the absolute limit. However, there were other qualities that she was more than happy to showcase and I confess that, on several cold, dark and lonely nights, these talents were freely exhibited to Mike Carpenter.

Not since ever-ready buxom Jane Middleton of the upper sixth, during a field trip to Harrogate, had I benefited from the education, experience and energy of a real woman who was lavish in her gift of what lay within her. Unfortunately, Kylie's reputation throughout the area garnered interest from other men and, as she was never inclined to deprive herself of male company, I obligingly stepped aside. When ultimately she returned to her roots twelve months ago, I failed to say goodbye, lose any sleep or shed a tear. Instead of looking for love in all the wrong places it was about time, as my granny Joan would say, that I found myself a nice young lady, settled down and embarked upon a meaningful relationship.

CHAPTER 4

Lifts from Strangers

On the final Saturday in September, I rose at the usual time, dressed quickly and went into the kitchen. Through the east-facing window, the sky was an iridescent blue; the sun was shining with all the single-hearted fervour that a late summer sun should but, in England, seldom does. Settled at the small rickety wooden table, I breakfasted modestly and contemplated the day ahead. At last I decided that, instead of making my routine visit to the local leisure centre for another strenuous session of intense physical abuse, I would go for a lengthy, energy-sapping run.

After changing into a plum-coloured T-shirt, flashy black shorts and white trainers, I snatched the bunch of keys from a hook above the door frame, kicked aside the unopened brown envelopes and left the apartment. I skipped eagerly down the outside steps and emerged into the warm, bright and spiritually disinfecting morning sunshine, where I spotted a trio of mute swans wheezing their way across the distant ranks of houses.

Setting out on the four-mile route, which took me all the way along Bolton Road, left at the Bricklayers' Arms and then in a semicircle back towards Primrose Avenue, I saw a frail old man tending his vegetables. He applauded encouragingly as I bounded energetically past the allotment, where two red admiral butterflies danced above a patch of drooping nettles and a kestrel hovered on wing tip. Jimmy was in his late fifties, bald as a grapefruit and with a weather-beaten face. He wore a pullover that looked like decaying cabbage, threadbare bottle-green corduroys and mud-spattered wellington boots. I had first encountered him in a nearby pub shortly after my relocation from Sheffield when, true to form, he had duped me into buying him a beer after I fell for one of his repertoire of card tricks. However, somewhere along the way the trials and tribulations of life seemed to have taken their toll and he had become a little sour. He constantly moaned that his ankle had gone, his knee had gone, his hip had gone; if he carried on any further, he would have ended up merely as a pair of spectacles resting on top of a prostate.

After taking a sharp left at the still-sleeping Brickies, my initial enthusiasm started to wane as my energy levels started to ebb. My stride shortened and I slackened to a gentle jog along Blackburn Road; this stretch was difficult to navigate due to an assortment of pram-pushing parents and scooter-riding children. I diverted into a narrow, rubble-strewn lane tangled with wild honeysuckle and blackthorn, which wound around the rear of a forbidding church, where I emerged once more onto the main road.

My progress was halted by an inconveniently parked hearse standing solemnly outside the front gates. Four men in shabby black coats leaned against the bonnet, smoking cigarettes cupped within their hands. The doors of the chapel opened and three bearers walked sombrely down the path, carrying the coffin lopsided on their shoulders. Resting on the lid was a small bouquet of pink roses arranged in the shape of a tennis racquet.

'Was he a player?' I asked respectfully of the chief undertaker, who had ketchup stains on the front of his shiny grey lapels.

'No, he was a spiv during the war,' he revealed disapprovingly and continued. 'Give them a hand with the box, will you, son? You're younger than us.' So, awash with sweat and conspicuous in my jogging gear, I did as I was asked as a bent shuffle of mourners dribbled out of the building. They watched with vague, watery eyes as the door to the yawning boot of the car was slammed shut and it slid away.

I resumed my exercise. When at long last I turned the corner and entered the home straight, I decelerated and chugged the remainder of the course. With bursting lungs and legs of jelly, I wobbled breathlessly up the steps and briefly watched a blue tit craftily working the branches of a ceanothus at the end of next door's garden, before gratefully entering the cool sanctuary of my apartment.

Luxuriating in a steaming hot bath, with foam up to my ears and the smell of sandalwood filling my nostrils, my muscles ached beyond belief. The pain gradually eased and my body started to relax, though my troublesome left foot still throbbed from a previous twist I had suffered during last week's overindulgence on an unforgiving treadmill in the health club.

I began to plan the remainder of the day. The first port of call was to the local betting office to place my weekly football accumulator before visiting the corner shop to pick up a few essentials. The rest of the afternoon was free until I met some work colleagues for a meal, which had been arranged for later in the evening.

When I went into the yeasty-smelling and chatter-filled bookies, I surveyed the busy scene before walking like John Wayne after dismounting from his horse to the green-fronted counter. The same two female members of staff from last week were processing the bets. Keen to be served by the younger and more attractive woman, I waited patiently in the longer queue. I was transfixed by people's willingness to dispose of their income. Fleetingly, I wondered how easy it might be to somehow rob or defraud this shop and escape with a large amount of cash before evaporating into the sun with a dusky beauty in tow, leaving behind all of my troubles.

'Hello,' I greeted the girl affably when it was my turn. 'How are you today?'

She faltered slightly before inclining her head and staring directly at me with piercing blue eyes. She issued a receipt together with my change before replying, while at the same time almost cracking a smile. 'I'm fine, thank you. How are you?'

'Very well,' I responded. 'It's very lively in here, isn't it?'

'Yes, it's an early start on the racing so everyone is rushing to place their bets.' I nodded understandingly before she added, 'Good luck with your bet later on.'

'Thanks, I'll need it.' I stepped away and made for the exit before a shout of 'Hey!' halted me in my tracks.

I turned my head sharply and saw the familiar figure of Biffo once again. He was leaning against the side of a roulette machine as his companion hopefully fed pound coins into the hungry, fixed-odds betting terminal. Trevor Derby was tall and thin, with a mane of thick coarse hair tied in a ponytail and a long, drawn face with prominent cheekbones. When he smiled he revealed a large set of upper teeth. The nickname 'Shergar' was given to him not only because of his similarity to the racehorse, but also because of his mysterious disappearances and the family surname. He listed slightly due to an ischium injury that he'd suffered while serving a twelve-month jail sentence.

Limping my way through the abandoned aspirations, dashed dreams and expired expectations which carpeted the unswept floor, I greeted them cheerfully. 'All right you two losers, how's it going?'

'Yeah, sweet, man, sweet,' Biffo replied nonchalantly. 'We saw you talking to that new bird again,' he added, while winking at his friend for support.

'Yeah,' Shergar joined in. 'I think you're in there, dude.'

'What, after only a couple of short verbal exchanges?' I protested vehemently, while feeling my cheeks start to flush.

'Yeah,' said Biffo. 'She doesn't even speak to us. She's a student or something. She looks well up for it, man.'

'That's right, those young, impressionable and gullible sorts are always gagging for it, innit,' Trevor concurred. This display of Neanderthal rhetoric served as a prime example of why we should never let morons have an opinion, let alone express one. Fortunately the subject of our conversation was out of earshot and busily assisting customers. I headed out of the library of luck, where the

42

gamblers quietly studied the form from Newmarket and Kempton Park.

After leaving, I hobbled slowly down the road before crossing from the sunlight into the shade provided by the imposing stone buildings on the other side. I went into the minimart and gathered a few provisions. My departure was delayed because a self-service till had been installed earlier that day. I waited behind an elderly lady with a frizzy perm as, in a misguided effort to embrace modern technology rather than stand in line with the technophobes, she began to scan her shopping. Unfortunately she couldn't find the barcodes on many of the products. The frantic jabbing of her finger on the unresponsive screen triggered an automated audio message of 'unidentified item in bagging area'. When she tried to pay for a bottle of wine, a question appeared, asking whether she was over eighteen. The voice continued, 'Please wait. An attendant will be with you shortly.' A youth, clad in a scarlet overall arrived and asked the pensioner for photo ID, which was required to complete the legal purchase of her Merlot. I learnt later that the first day of the self-service till was not a tremendous success as most customers had needed intervention, and one feeble gentleman needed resuscitation.

Later, after dozing fitfully on the couch in my home, I woke just in time to see the football scores appear on the television. Gazing out of the sitting room window, I saw that the beautiful weather of earlier had given way to a grey sky with menacing heavy clouds rolling in on a freshening westerly that stripped the leaves from the trees.

I dressed slowly before leaving around eight o'clock to drive the relatively short distance and meet my work colleagues. The weather had taken a turn for the worse and declined into a typical autumnal Manchester evening. Motoring vigilantly along the puddle-strewn road, I was surprised to see the vivacious girl from the betting shop standing alone at the vandalised, bunk-off bus stop. An indescribable thrill passed through me as I slowed down, pulled in and pipped my horn loudly. I lowered the window, swallowed hard and shouted in an effort to be heard above the roar of the passing traffic, 'Come on, get in. I'll give you a lift.'

Her five foot four frame was huddled against what remained of the broken shelter. She was zipped into a coconut-brown suede jacket; her right hand clutched a blue-and-white spotted umbrella which acted as a shield against the elements. Her bag was slung over the other shoulder. At first, she did not seem to recognise me.

'Come on, get in, I'll give you a lift,' I repeated.

She shuffled forward tentatively, lowered her head and peered inside the car. Recognition spread across her face. 'Oh, it's you!'

She wrenched open the door and scrambled in while desperately wrestling with the unfurled, dripping brolly which stubbornly refused to collapse. Eventually, she slammed the door shut and clicked her seat belt into position. The smell of her damp clothing was eclipsed by the heady scent of her perfume.

'Do you often accept lifts from strangers?' I joked as I accelerated away.

'Why, are you strange?' she replied, while staring ahead through the rain-slicked screen.

'Oh yes, very,' I said, before glancing sideways and grinning cheekily.

A period of awkward but polite small talk followed.

She flicked away a solitary raindrop which was creeping steadily down her nose and asked, 'Where are you going?'

'I'm just meeting some people from work. We're all going to the Print Works for something to eat,' I answered.

'That sounds nice. I've been there; it's good fun,' she remarked.

'Where do you want dropping off?' I enquired.

'Just behind the Golden Lion would be awesome,' she said.

'The Golden Lion?' I echoed. 'Is that the one near the halls of residence?'

'Yes,' she confirmed while adjusting her fringe.

'What are you studying?'

'I'm a second-year law student,' she disclosed proudly.

'Very good.' I was full of admiration.

After an interval she enquired, 'What's your name?'

'Mike Carpenter,' I responded. 'Yours is Sandy, according to your name tag.'

'Yes, it's Sandy Gibson.' Another spell of quiet passed as we dredged for things to talk about. At last she asked, 'What do you do for a living?'

'I'm only a humble salesman for a double glazing firm. It's nothing special and I'm thinking of moving on,' I declared.

A further three tongue-tied minutes passed. As I turned down the side of the Lion, she said, 'If you drop me off here, I'll walk the rest of the way. That'll be mega.'

'But it's still raining,' I protested. 'I'll take you right to the door, it's no problem.'

'No, here is fine. Drop me right here,' she insisted.

After thanking me politely she jumped out, slammed the passenger door and scurried off without a backward glance. I watched wistfully as, framed against the drizzle and silhouetted by the yellow street lights, she moved towards an alleyway, which divided the two accommodation blocks. The aroma of her fragrance lingered and I started to experience an unfamiliar feeling in the pit of my stomach. Was that the sound of Venus's hunting horn I could hear?

Keen to check on her safety, I slid level with the narrow entrance and stared anxiously down the poorly illuminated passageway. But the beguiling beauty, who was about to play a major role in my life, had already dissolved into the rainy night.

Chapter 5

That's Torn It

During the following week, a co-worker offered me a ticket to watch God's own football team play a home match against Arsenal. This unexpected golden opportunity was not to be missed as it was the first fixture of the season which I was able to attend. Since the well-deserved retirement of the legendary Sir Alex Ferguson, United had failed to achieve the levels of performance demanded by the 75,000 faithful disciples who paid unwavering homage at Old Trafford. Due to satellite television commitments, the kick-off was scheduled for 12.45 on the Saturday so I went to the leisure centre earlier than usual before visiting the bookmakers.

When I went in, I saw Sandy sitting alone behind the counter. Boosted by testosterone, I approached boldly as she lifted her head, set down her pen and smiled brightly. 'Good morning,' I greeted cheerfully.

'Hi there. You are early today,' she responded chirpily.

'Yes, I'm going to watch the footie with a friend,' I declared.

'Awesome. Is it the Reds?' she asked, with twinkling eyes.

'Of course, who else? There is only one decent team in Manchester,' I replied and winked.

'I know very little about the sport. Are they the only club around here?' she enquired innocently before handing over my receipt.

'Thanks,' I said. 'They are the only side that matters in this particular city,' I asserted before heading rapidly for the exit.

As I reached the frosted glass door, I was struck by a sudden flash of inspiration. Glancing around the shop, I noticed there was only one other customer. Appearing strangely out of place, he was a shifty-looking man in a loud suit who was pretending to be immersed in playing the blackjack machine while sneakily peering around as though he was casing the joint or expecting something to happen. I remained vigilant until the he left then, yielding to an irrational impulse, I snatched a blank betting slip from a transparent Perspex holder which was glued to the wall. I tore it in half and, using a stubby pencil, quickly scribbled my phone number together with a brief message that read: 'Mike. Call me sometime.' Shaking with nerves, I crept back to the cashier and slipped the scrap of paper under the protective glass.

Without altering her facial expression, she picked up the note, read it and crumpled the slip into a ball before thrusting it securely into her pocket. Unaccustomed to such acts of impulsiveness, I waited, fearing some kind of negative backlash or confidence-crushing rejection. She leaned forward and whispered, 'Cool. I'll call you later.'

Driving through the heavy lunchtime traffic which dribbled along the Mancunian Way, as the sun cowered behind soaring banks of clouds, I speculated on the length of time it might take for her to succumb to temptation and ring my mobile. Did she simply toss the scrunched paper into a rubbish bin as soon as I left, considering me to be just another sad loser, or would she want to get to know me better? If she took the former view, I would be highly embarrassed and unlikely to set foot in the place again; however, if she adopted the latter approach, it might be the beginning of something very special indeed. I hoped she would make a quick decision.

The game was very nondescript and petered out into a goalless draw. United's performance was, like so many others that season, comparable to an experience of kissing your sister: technically correct but lacking in passion or excitement. As I made my way to the apartment, I received an unsolicited call from an unfamiliar number. Fearing it was a call centre eager to know whether I had been mis-sold PPI or had been involved in an accident which was not my fault I barked impatiently, 'Hello.' My finger hovered above the disconnect button.

'Is that Mike?' enquired a friendly female voice. From the softness of the tone and slight northern lilt I knew instantly who it was.

'It is,' I confirmed, breaking into a broad smile.

'It's Sandy from the bookies.'

'Oh hi,' I replied, feigning surprise. 'How's it going?'

'Everything is fine. I'm just having a quick break and after this morning I thought I'd give you a buzz.'

'No problem,' I said. 'It's nice to hear from you.'

'I've been wondering,' she continued tentatively, 'if you're free, do you want to go for a drink later on?'

'Yes, absolutely,' I replied keenly. 'When and where?'

'Around eight o'clock?' she suggested.

'Tonight is good for me. I have no plans. Where shall we meet?'

'Can you pick me up at the bus shelter near the shop where we met last time?'

'OK, I'll see you then.'

'Cool. I'll look forward to it,' she concluded.

Filled with elation, I punched the air.

Heartened by the invitation, I soaked in the bath and reflected on the possibilities which might arise from spending some quality time with a captivating young woman. Some time had elapsed since my last steady girlfriend and I had started to question whether I was still capable of holding an interesting level of conversation with a woman without wanting to drag her off to the bedroom. Would I be able to portray myself as witty and entertaining and display a good sense of humour which, it seemed, most women required? Not since melon-breasted Lisa Battersby dispossessed me of my innocence behind the school science block shortly after my sixteenth birthday had I felt so nervous. Could this be it, could this be the big one?

In due course, after the tension and stiffness in my body gradually subsided, I finished bathing and dressed in a black roll-neck jumper, brand new trousers and matching, comfortable shoes. Banishing the jitters and doubling as the Milk Tray man, I called in at the nearby minimart in order to purchase a small gift for my date, where I noticed that the pride and joy which was the self-service till stood alone, silent and unused. While I paid for a pricey box of luxury chocolates, a stout female assistant with a robust face, harelip and smelling of pear drops lisped that a frustrated and inebriated customer had earlier rendered the equipment useless by launching an unprovoked, furious and sustained attack upon it.

Wearing a calf-length coat and brown boots, Sandy was already waiting when I pulled into the bus lay-by five minutes later. Across the road I spotted a grey van with buckled wheels brooding forlornly on the forecourt of a filling station. After I gallantly opened the passenger door, she climbed into the car. As she twisted her body to fasten the seatbelt, I could see that she had applied a little makeup and smelt faintly but pleasantly of menthol vapours.

'Hi, how are you doing? You look really nice?' I said amiably.

'Fine, thank you. I'm OK now that my shift has finished,' she answered wearily and yawned.

'Have you been busy, then?'

'Yes, it's been manic.' She puffed out her cheeks and tried to relax in her seat.

I reached forward and took the slim, rectangular present from the dashboard and passed it to her. 'Something for you,' I said, grinning widely.

'For me?' she squealed excitedly, before eagerly tearing off the wrapper. 'Lush. They are my favourites.' Instead of opening the box and offering the contents, though, she tucked them into her handbag, which rested on her lap.

'Where do you want to go?' I asked, feeling rather pleased with myself.

'Let's have a drink in the Golden Lion, near the halls

of residence,' she proposed.

'Good idea.' We spent the rest of the short journey exchanging accounts of how we had spent our day as a fine rain started to fall from an already darkening sky.

Predictably enough for a weekend in a student stronghold, the pub was heaving with humanity. The adjacent Barley Mow was holding a karaoke session and anyone who didn't want to listen to bad impersonations of Frank Sinatra or Gloria Gaynor found themselves in the Lion.

I offered Sandy my arm and escorted her into a large and stifling room. We ordered our drinks and settled in a quieter spot near the window, next to an old man who was hunched over an untouched orangeade; he appeared to be reading his fortune while prodding at his ear with a spent match.

After an initial few minutes of sharing dry roasted peanuts and shy smiles, we began to swap details of our personal lives. Sandy divulged that she was born and bred in Shrewsbury. She never knew her father and was raised by her mother as an only child but, sadly, her mother had died from cancer three years earlier and there were no other relatives. Revealing this information caused Sandy some distress; her eyes grew moist, her lips began to tremble and she bowed her head, apparently unwilling to discuss the subject any further.

She told me that she had moved to Manchester two years ago to study law at the university; her friend Jessica, who originated from Sussex, was on the same course and they shared a two-bedroomed flat. Sandy's musical tastes included anything by Rihanna or Jessie J, she liked films featuring Kate Winslet or Meg Ryan and enjoyed Indian and Italian food. In addition, she tried to visit the gym at least twice a week. She joked that her main ambitions were to settle down one day, have children and become filthy rich.

Our heart to heart was rudely interrupted, however, when a young member of the drug-taking fraternity sidled up to our table. His pitted face, dilated pupils and toothless grin hinted at his terrible habit, while the scabby hands, filthy fingernails and tiny puncture marks on his arms added fuel to our suspicions. His baggy, stained T-shirt depicted a hippy smoking a joint and a slogan which pleaded *Decriminalise Cannabis*. He carried a bulging carrier bag from which he started to remove a collection of toiletries. 'Hey man, do you want any of these?' he asked. 'I've got deodorant, razor blades, aftershaves, all that kind of stuff. What do you want, man?'

'No. Go away, I don't want anything,' I insisted firmly.

'Well, I've got something for your wife,' he said, undeterred. He rummaged in his bag and extracted several bottles of expensive-looking perfume along with a selection of elegant watches, which he set out in front of Sandy.

'No, we don't want any of it. Shut up and shove off,' she said scornfully.

'What do you need, then?' he persisted irritatingly. 'I can get you anything. Just name it and I'll go for it right now.'

'No, thank you,' I repeated and waved dismissively.

'All right man, chill out. I didn't mean to mither you or violate your space,' he apologised as he put the stuff back in his bag. 'I was just trying to get a few quid for a bit of gear.' He slithered away in search of his next victim.

An hour later Sandy noticed the clock above the bar, drained her fourth gin and banged her glass down heavily. She leapt to her feet and announced, 'I should get going. Thanks for the drink; it's been good fun.'

'You're welcome,' I said. I slid across to help with her coat but as I did so, something seemed to pluck at the seat of my trousers. I felt behind me and discovered that I could comfortably insert a finger into a rent in the material. I looked back and saw to my horror the tip of a broken spring emerging from the upholstery. Why me, I thought? Why did I have to tear my new trousers at this precise moment?

Sandy viewed the incident as extremely amusing. 'You can't go outside like that,' she giggled. 'You'll have to stay until closing time.' Thankfully the length of my jacket covered any potential embarrassment.

It was still drizzling in the deserted and shadowy car park, so I offered to drive Sandy the few hundred yards to her accommodation. 'No thanks, it's cool. I'll walk,' she insisted. She leaned forward, gently pinched my cheek and kissed me. 'Laters,' she whispered and skipped away.

I watched forlornly as she blended in with the dark and I became aware of a strange sense of isolation taking hold of me. The excitement and thrill generated in the last few hours had been replaced by a sense of anticlimax. The evening was over, she had gone home alone and, disappointingly, she had not invited me back for coffee.

I had a strong desire to run after her, throw my arms around her neck and reassure her that everything would be all right for ever and ever. Spontaneity is not a part of my nature, however, so instead I trudged miserably to my car with a sinking feeling of 'After the Lord Mayor's

Show'.

Obviously in a situation like this, where two souls are seeking salvation, it is impossible to guess – let alone know – what the other person is thinking. When I reached the car, however, my phone vibrated with a text message which read: 'Thanks Mike for a nice evening, we must do it again, ring me soon.'

My heart leapt and I replied swiftly: 'I also had a good time, I'll call you tomorrow. Take care.'

Intoxicated with happiness and staring blankly at the illuminated screen, I believed that hope had been restored once more and during that peaceful night, her laughter echoed through my erotic dreams.

CHAPTER 6

Bedtime

It was a dark foggy morning at the gloomier end of October, when the days shorten and the clocks fall back, as I wandered once again to the hostel of hope. Surprisingly, the doorway was blocked completely by a couple of thickset, sweating bruisers who were focused on repairing a glass panel. In an effort to be heard above the roar of the passing traffic, I coughed loudly and caught their attention. They straightened in unison, spun around and looked at me, surprised. 'Excuse me, lads, can I just squeeze past and come in?' I asked courteously.

The larger and older man replied in a strong Scouse accent, 'Sorry, mate. We're just fixing this, like.' He stepped aside and beckoned me into the dinginess of the shop.

Inside I surveyed the male-dominated scene then bustled across the grey-tiled floor to Sandy's position at the counter. 'Hello, you,' I said softly, as I pushed my long odds accumulator under the shield.

'Oh, hi there. How are you?' she responded warmly after taking a quick slurp from a can of fizzy drink.

'I'm fine, thanks. What's the problem with the door?' I enquired.

'We had an attempted break-in overnight,' Sandy explained.

'Really!' I exclaimed. 'Did they take anything?'

'No. Fortunately the alarm was raised and the police arrived in the nick of time.' She pointed at the glaziers. 'That pair are supposed to be mending the bottom section but they're taking their time and keep demanding cups of tea, with sugar and biscuits.'

She gave me a stamped receipt. After looking over my shoulder, I edged forward and asked hopefully, 'Are you still on for tonight?'

'Yes,' she mouthed. 'Meet me in our usual spot around eight o'clock.' Checking to ensure that our secret was still safe, she shot a sideways glance at Scottish Marjorie, who was thankfully paying no heed to us but was engrossed in serving another customer and exchanging bawdy banter.

Since our nervous first date, Sandy and I had met on four other occasions for a drink. This evening was to be our first meal together and I had booked a table at an exclusive restaurant in a salubrious part of town.

Brightening at the forthcoming prospect of an evening with an alluring female, I had a strong desire to sharpen my image and I rashly decided to go shopping for some new clothes. Reluctant to drive into the city centre at the weekend because of the lack of parking – and the ridiculous costs if you did find a space – I decided to take the bus. The number twenty-nine was packed with a cross-section of society, ranging from young children yelling on their teenaged mothers' laps, to unwashed pensioners harping on to anyone within earshot about the 'good old days'.

We inched jerkily along the crowded route, stopping to pick up and drop off passengers, observe traffic lights, halt at empty pedestrian crossings and brake sharply to negotiate tight corners. The interminable experience seemed to take longer than the publication of the Chilcot Report into the Iraq War.

The antiperspirant-avoiding and razor-reluctant rabble who sat far too close for comfort, mixed with the acridness of people experiencing bladder issues and the eggy pong of IBS sufferers, created a truly obnoxious cocktail of stench which even the eye-stinging pungency of cheap perfume was unable to disguise. The reek of stale cigarettes and last night's booze compounded my discomfort while, noisily along the back seat of the boneshaker, a posse of One Directioners with challenging behaviour screamed, spat and swore indiscriminately and unashamedly like cretins on some type of medication. Upstairs on the top deck, God only knew what hellish devilment was afoot. Scowling gently and staring hard through the grubby and streaked windows, it was barely possible to see the rows of boarded-up retailers interspersed by takeaways, loan sharks and tattoo parlours, which fur Britain's modern high streets, as the rain began to fall from a forbidding sky.

At long last the journey ended when we pulled into the terminus and the noisy passengers disembarked from the depressing, dirty diesel guzzler. Standing briefly on the litter-strewn pavement and gulping greedily at the fresh, damp afternoon air, I headed off to the traditional barbers, with its polished wooden planks, fine-toothed steel combs and slim packets of requisites before going in search of some new glad rags.

Swerving the multitude of chuggers, I mooched around for over an hour among the thronging hordes and various outlets housed within the Arndale Centre, until, with thinning patience, my attention was drawn to a half-price sale where I decided to purchase a stylish white shirt, tight-fitting chinos and a pair of leather lace-up brogues before, keen to remain on time and anxious not to repeat the foolish decision of earlier, I hailed a cab and made my way back home.

As the taxi lumbered its fifteen-minute ride through the narrow, clogged arteries and fume-choked lungs of the city, the driver conversed coherently on several topics rather than resorting to indecipherable grunting. After alighting, and as a reward for this unexpected distraction, I gave him a generous two-pound tip on top of his clocked fare.

Sometime later, I sat on the edge of the bed clipping my fingernails and contemplating the state of our developing relationship. Sandy and I seemed to be getting along very well and appeared to be on the same wavelength. We listened to similar types of music, watched the same films and took pleasure in all types of entertainment; additionally we both had a wicked sense of humour and enjoyed the same taste in food. The one thing we lacked in common was a passion for sport; Sandy knew nothing about it and cared even less, while I knew all about it and cared deeply. Who said opposites don't attract?

It is paramount in any new relationship not only to respect each other's preferences, opinions and views, but also to identify some mutual ground. The fundamentals are communication and trust; without both you have nothing. Now that the initial awkwardness had worn off, we were beginning to move forward and everything in the garden looked rosy.

Dressed in the clothing I'd bought earlier, I wriggled my feet into the unyielding shoes and tied the laces loosely before sliding precariously into the lounge. My eyes were drawn to a painting given to me by my parents as a moving-in present. Hanging on the wall behind the settee, it was a large sporting picture of a huntsman, proudly displaying the results of a successful day's hunting. Strategically positioned, it replaced the previous bizarre depiction of Elvis at the Last Supper, which had been left by the previous tenant.

Preparation is the key to success so I hobbled gingerly to the bathroom, liberally applied some expensive aftershave to my cheeks and, smelling like a desert flower, slipped on my coat. With a sense of schoolboy excitement, I departed for what I sincerely hoped would be an amazing evening.

I glided silently alongside Sandy as she neared the graffiti-scarred bus stop, pulled up and pipped the horn sharply. She jumped, as though startled by the unexpected sound, before regaining her composure, turning quickly and recognising the car. Giving me a bewitching smile, she climbed in. I noticed that her face was carefully made-up, hair recently washed and a faint whiff of scent teased my nostrils.

'You look fabulous,' I complimented her. 'How are you? Have you had a good day?'

'Thank you for the compliment. Yes, I'm fine. It's been mega-busy,' she replied, glancing at me.

'Did you get changed at work?' I enquired.

'No, I finished at six o'clock and went home to get

ready.'

'Oh, I see,' I said. 'I thought you were wearing different clothes from this morning.'

'I decided to make the effort if we are fine dining.' She giggled and added, 'I see you pushed the boat out.'

'Yes, you try your best,' I replied, acting cool. We chatted casually for the remainder of the journey before crossing a shallow packhorse bridge and arriving at Giuseppe's Trattoria precisely on time.

The triple-rosette-awarded restaurant, displaying prices high enough to cause a nosebleed, was charming and cosy. It held no more than forty diners and its lofty reputation was such that it was preferable to book at least a fortnight in advance. On this special occasion I was quick off the mark, following a nod and a wink from a work colleague who had told me earlier in the week that she couldn't take up her reservation.

A tall, wiry waiter with Mediterranean features ushered us discreetly to our table, which was covered by a stiff white cloth that was embroidered with patterns of the Italian flag. On either side was a deep-red, richly upholstered straight-backed chair; in the middle, an attractive light hung like a stalactite from the whitewashed ceiling, providing a soft illumination which only increased the already romantic atmosphere.

When Sandy removed her wrap and draped it nonchalantly over the back of her chair, she revealed a three-quarter-length yellow silk dress, which rustled as she moved. There were spaghetti straps over her pale shoulders and she was wearing no bra; skin-toned stockings were visible above her gold shoes and a thin silver chain elegantly adorned her left wrist. She had clearly spent a lot of time and trouble getting ready and, as she stood gazing affectionately up at me, I considered randily that, aged in her mid twenties with an angelic face, swimming-pool eyes and a body with all the right curves in all the right places, she looked snatched. When she opened her kissable mouth to speak, I could have been arrested for what I was thinking.

'Let's sit down,' she suggested and, as though in a wonderful, wonderful dream, I acquiesced.

The waiter took out a box of matches and lit the candle before we ordered an immodestly priced white wine which, as the sommelier predicted, possessed a light and crisp timbre, before perusing the extensive menu which boasted that all of the products used were locally sourced and delivered fresh on a daily basis. Several minutes later, I perceived from her body language that she was starting to relax as she polished off the lion's share of the first bottle of wine. A second was ordered with the antipasti and a third shortly after. As the evening progressed, the increasingly slurred conversation ebbed and flowed. We inadvertently brushed fingers during some animated discussion, occasionally knocked knees under the table and delighted in each other's company. I noticed her habit of raising a hand and fiddling seductively with her fringe. After blighting our first date by behaving like a couple of strangers standing in a post office queue, the awkward, tongue-tied silences were now draining away.

Changing the subject entirely while we sipped our liqueur coffees, Sandy asked, 'Have you ever been recognised in the street?'

Briefly taken aback, I pondered on this peculiar question before wittily replying, 'Only when I see myself in a shop window.'

She dwelt momentarily on my answer then said, 'That's not funny.' After a minor hesitation, she started again. 'Actually, on reflection, that's a smashing joke.' We laughed then she tried again. 'Have you ever done a bungee jump?'

'Well,' I replied thoughtfully, 'I have zoomed in and out of Google Earth very quickly. Does that count?' She stared with puzzled interest and nodded politely.

After a minute or two, she began to caress my foot with hers and, exposing more cleavage by leaning towards me, whispered, 'What are you like in bed?'

I responded cheekily, 'I can hold my own.'

She remained seated for a moment then, without warning, pushed back her chair and sprang to her feet. 'Come on, then, let's go and find out,' she declared.

For a moment it was as if every other person in the crowded room had ceased to exist. Oddly, for an impoverished student who only worked part time, she insisted on settling the bill with cash. In turn, I left a small gratuity before, with impure motives and floating on a lake of lust, we left.

Disregarding my parked car, we climbed into a waiting taxi and headed for the apartment as our relationship gathered momentum. Sitting quietly, but as of one mind, in the strange-smelling, brake-squealing and tension-riddled darkness, neither of us wanted to speak. We could barely look at each other because of the massive expectation of what was to come. Sandy took my hand and held it tightly before breaking the silence. 'Do we need to stop for anything?' she asked, swallowing hard and thinking responsibly.

By now my throat was Sahara-dry, my heart was thumping and my mind was racing. It took me all of my strength to murmur, 'No, I bought a pint of milk at lunchtime.' This poor effort to ease the tension did not impress her or elicit a flicker of emotion; I think by that stage she was preparing herself for an unforgettable and outstanding night of passion.

CHAPTER 7

Big Brother is Watching

After the night of exhilarating delight which we had shared Sandy and I had, over the last month, begun to spend an increasing amount of time together. We seemed very comfortable in each other's company and the awkwardness and inhibitions of the past had become just distant memories. Routinely we met during the week to have a drink or enjoy a meal, while Saturday evenings were spent relaxing at my apartment. This greatly anticipated, pleasurable arrangement continued unabated until the final weekend in November.

Drawing up in front of my property, I noticed Kieran's dented vehicle parked at an inconsiderate angle. Burly and boisterous, he sprang from the saloon, slammed the door and rushed over to greet me. 'How do, our kid?' he said and gave me a rib-crushing hug.

'Yeah, I'm all right bro,' I responded. 'Give me a lift with these bags from the boot of the car. I need to get the shopping indoors.'

My brother was two years older than me, about six feet tall, strongly built, with thick coarse hair, big brown eyes and a rugged, clean-shaven face. He wore a navy sweatshirt emblazoned with a picture of an owl heading a football and a message which read *It's Wise to Support Wednesday*. His jeans matched his brand new black trainers.

Kieran was employed as an electrician by a local company but I would struggle to describe him as a bright spark. I always considered that he was tuned into a lower frequency than most and when I was younger he had tried to bully me because of my superior intellectual skills. But, as we passed through adolescence and into manhood, the brotherly bond had become stronger. At times though, his behaviour could be boorish, selfish and less than fraternal – especially where women were involved. He was, like the majority of men, ruled by a part of his anatomy other than his brain.

When we had lugged the groceries up the stairs and indoors, my brother said in his own inimitable way, 'Bloody hell, who is all this booze and scran for?'

'I told you the other morning when we spoke on the phone. I am hosting my girlfriend and her flatmate for supper.'

'Oh yeah,' he recalled, desperately searching among the cobwebs of his memory bank. 'I forgot about that.' After a slight pause he added, 'So we are not going chasing skirt then, or hunting for cougars?'

'Definitely not,' I confirmed, while squeezing the comestibles into the already well-stocked fridge and cupboard. 'Sandy is bringing her friend Jessica around for a drink and something to eat.'

'Oh,' exclaimed Kieran, gaining interest. 'What's Jessica like, then?'

'I've not met her yet but I've been told that she's very articulate, extremely highbrow and too classy for a big dope like you,' I joked. Then I added, 'Sometimes I envy you. The big issues and weighty problems of the day never seem to cloud your thoughts.' He just laughed falsely and gave me a two-fingered salute.

I had been surprised when, earlier that week, my brother had telephoned me to accept an invitation to stay. I had invited him back in August and we had not spoken during the intervening period.

Sometime later, we were lounging on the sofa and half-watching the National Hunt Racing from Haydock Park, where the timber-topping and hedge-hopping warriors battled bravely on the good-to-soft going at the Lancashire track. 'If your chance came, would you take it?' asked Kieran arbitrarily, as he carried on playing *Game of Thrones* on his mobile.

'What do you mean by that?' I asked, raising an eyebrow.

'Well,' he began slowly and sat upright, 'the chances are we'll never be able to afford a gee-gee, buy a Roller or own a holiday pad unless we get loads of wonga from somewhere, and the possibility of us doing that is zero. So, we will need to do a bank, screw a wages van or work a scam to get enough readies to set us up for life. If an opportunity came up, have you got the bottle to take it?'

I thought for a moment before sliding to the edge of the settee and declaring, 'I'm not sure. It's hard to say because it's a hypothetical question. But I agree with you – in order to be comfortable, rich and never have to work again, you need a stroke of luck or to devise and execute a cunning plan.'

He nodded thoughtfully in agreement, clicked off the app and suggested, 'Shall we go for a pint and shoot some pool?'

'Yes, OK,' I agreed. 'We can't be back too late because I need to cook the meal and get everything ready for tonight.'

'Come on then, you big wuss.' He sprang energetically to his feet.

The weather was nondescript as we walked the short distance to the Bricklayers' Arms. As we passed the allotments that skirted the right-hand side of the busy road, I noticed a solitary old man, standing in a fennel patch outside his recently creosoted wooden shed. This figure, with the roseate and weather-beaten complexion of a man who spent a good deal of his time dunging the vegetables in his North Country garden, was steadily puffing on a pipe. He raised his left thumb in acknowledgement, as a thin skein of smoke drifted idly up into the sky on a light breeze. Out of politeness, I waved back to the flat-capped old-timer who stamped his dirty boots in an effort to dislodge the claggy mud. 'Who's that?' asked my brother.

'I've no idea,' I replied. 'But he seems to recognise me from somewhere. He may have seen me in the bookies.'

'Oh no,' protested Kieran. 'You don't still go in those places wasting your money, do you? It's a mug's game.'

'Only on a Saturday. I like to have a football bet. We're not the same; you are as tight as a trumpeter's cheeks. And it's your round when we get to the pub,' I insisted.

We were greeted by a murmur like someone breaking wind in a library as we entered the relatively empty Brickies.

A few of the regulars were in the taproom. My brother was in the process of ordering two pints at the bar when I was forced to turn around by a heavy but affectionate thump on the shoulder, delivered by big Freddy 'with a y'.

'Now then, son, what are you doing in here?' he asked with a Lancashire twang.

'I've just brought my brother in to have a couple of beers and teach him a lesson in playing stripes and spots,' I joked, while shaking Freddy's nicotine-stained, sausage-fingered hand.

Freddy said, 'Come on then, I'll play you. Don't forget the winner stays on and doesn't pay for the next game.'

The walls of the room were covered in yellow plaid wallpaper. A glass-fronted display cabinet, mounted in the corner, proudly displayed various cups, shields and trophies redolent of past glories. A cherry-coloured padded bench shaped like a horseshoe, surrounded a nest of beer-stained wooden tables with matching low stools at one end of the bar while a battered games table, in desperate need of re-covering, dominated the other.

A pair of scruffy scrotes, in back-to-front baseball caps, sat in the corner under the flickering television near the window, drinking cheap cider and occasionally going out of the fire door in order to share 'a fat one'. An old codger sat across from them, scratching himself methodically, tapping his feet; he was obviously the worse for drink, as he attempted to read the *Racing Post* while holding it upside down. Four other middle-aged men sat playing cards for money; the tolerant landlord turned a blind eye to their gambling, a deaf ear to the swearing and said nothing to anyone.

During the next couple of hours hardly any fresh faces

enter the sticky-floored, stale-smelling saloon. Those who did, along with the long-stay patients, appeared to be fascinated by my sibling. I suppose his ornithological sweatshirt acted as an icebreaker; certainly his risqué jokes encouraged them and his intellect was pitched at their level.

Around five o'clock, big Freddy 'with a y' drifted off for his usual rough shag and then his tea and 'our kid' joined in with a friendly game of pontoon. Several deals passed off peacefully for small stakes until, having risked all of one pound, Kieran argued with the banker that, because thirteen plus nine equals twenty-one, he was entitled to be paid. A heated row started with the other players before his short fuse lit. In a fit of rage, Kieran snatched his drink, tossed it over the seafood man and delivered a thudding blow flush on the jaw of the surprised milkman. As the table was overturned, the stools upended and the pots smashed on the tiled floor, the foursome descended into a whirlwind of aftershave, a writhing mass of limbs and a tirade of cursing. On the point of lending a brotherly hand, I noticed the ex-Speedway-riding landlord limp from behind the bar brandishing a cricket bat like a Samurai sword.

'Get up and get out,' he roared, waving the weapon threateningly at Kieran and me. My brother, grinning and winking, disentangled himself and rose from the melee; he was studded by glass, soaked in lager and smeared with someone's claret.

'Get him out,' insisted the proprietor, pointing at me. 'You are both barred. Don't ever come in here again.' The opposition, who remained drinking in the spit-and-sawdust, bizarrely bade us a hearty farewell. With no hard feelings, they said they hoped that we would return again soon. This show of bonhomie appeared to signal that, despite the fracas and because we had spent some time in their company, we were now fast-tracked into their posse. I'm certain the natives viewed the incident as one of bridge-building that had brought us together but I viewed it as erecting a barrier which would keep us apart. I would definitely not be returning.

Hurrying home in a rapidly descending pea-souper Kieran, fortified by four pints and a brief skirmish, asked, 'So these two birds tonight then, ... yours is Sandy, which leaves me to have a crack at Jessica. Is that right?'

Full of outrage, I stopped abruptly and issued a verbal warning. 'No, there is to be none of that kind of smutty talk or that sort of behaviour. It's going to be a pleasant, sophisticated evening, with intelligent and stimulating conversation. Is that clear?' I wagged an admonishing finger.

'Yeah, but if she's single, breathing and up for it, it's worth a go,' Kieran said lasciviously.

'Jessica currently doesn't have a boyfriend,' I confirmed. 'But don't try anything. I know what you're like. She is classy, but you'll throw your leg over any old piece of filth that moves.'

'I don't care if they move or not,' he responded, only partially joking, before continuing, 'Are you sleeping with Sandy now?'

'We have become good friends,' I replied evasively.

He tried again. 'But have you slept with her?'

'It's none of your business. Anyway, she's not staying tonight because you're sleeping in the lounge. And don't tell Mum and Dad anything,' I warned.

'I see,' he sneered, while grinning like a Cheshire cat.

The two law students presented themselves at about eight o'clock. After hanging their bags and coats in the cupboard, the introductions were made. Jessica was around five feet eight inches tall, with narrow hips; her hair was long and golden and cascaded over her shoulders, while her green eyes sparkled with life. She wore a purple T-shirt which proclaimed *Brighton Rocks* in white lettering across her full breasts. She seemed to be bouncy, warm-hearted and very intelligent. Sandy was dressed distractingly in a tight, peach-coloured blouse which accentuated her slim waist, and a pair of elegant taupe trousers. Her hair had been washed and her clear blue eyes were full of anticipation. She looked ravishing.

In my opinion the evening was an unmitigated triumph. Both the hastily prepared spaghetti bolognese and cheese-topped garlic bread were quickly devoured by the famished students and the unappreciative electrician. Busy in the kitchen but blessed with acute hearing, I heard the girls start to giggle and talk flatteringly about me while Kieran answered a call of nature. 'Mike is really nice,' Jessica said. 'He's good-looking and seems very kind. You're very lucky to have met someone like that,' she added in a cut-glass accent.

'I know,' Sandy concurred. 'He's very generous and easy-going. I'm so happy and tremendously excited. I think that this might be the one.'

'If you feel that way, hang on tightly. Treat him well and be truthful. You must reveal your secrets and, if he's as good as we think, he'll understand. I hope it works out for you after all you've been through during these past few years. You deserve some good luck,' Jessica whispered.

'I can't tell him. He'll dump me for sure. There's too much to lose,' Sandy replied before they filled their glasses and clinked the rims. A half-dozen bottles of cheap red plonk did not survive past the dessert of strawberry cheesecake and my reserve supply of canned lager was polished off before the girls left in the early hours of Sunday.

In an effort to hide any clue to our embryonic relationship, Sandy kept an expressionless face as she prepared to leave. I watched with a pang of jealousy when she leaned in to Kieran and kissed him full on the mouth. Jessica's squiffy adieu was more formal; she shook hands courteously, thanked me profusely and prematurely wished me a 'Happy Christmas' before scrambling into the back of a black cab with her flatmate and rattling off into the fog-wrapped streets.

When I went back inside, I asked my brother what he thought of Sandy. 'She's all right,' he replied in a non-committal fashion. 'But she is too smart for me. Where did you meet her?'

'She works weekends at the betting shop. I think she is amazing,' I said.

'Yeah, yeah, she's all right,' he said begrudgingly. 'Her face seems a bit familiar.'

'I doubt it,' I replied. 'She was born and bred in Shrewsbury. Her mum died three years ago and she has no surviving family nor any close friends. She moved here shortly afterwards to study for a law degree at the university. Although we've only been together for a few weeks I feel that the relationship is flourishing. We're growing closer and her affection for me seems genuine. I think this could be exactly what I am searching for, something special, the big one.'

Glancing across to the settee, I saw that he was sodden with drink and spark out.

CHAPTER 8

From West to East

Three weeks before Christmas, I took my car to Alan's Autos for its annual service. The garage was a family-run business, located on an industrial estate approximately a mile from my home and overlooked by a block of residential flats. As I arrived on that frosty Saturday morning, a troop of grease monkeys were labouring intensively on other vehicles, exhaling clouds of breath into the freezing air, occasionally rubbing their gloveless hands together and stamping their boots in an effort to keep warm.

The owner's son was tall, well-nourished and needed the services of a trichologist. He sported a red name tag on his dirty grey overall which read 'Dave'. Standing in the cramped, windowless office, where a gas heater belched and gurgled noisily in the corner, he scratched my details into a dog-eared ledger and announced, 'This won't be ready until tomorrow dinner time, pal. Is that all right?'

'Do you work on Sunday?' I quizzed.

'Yes. This time of year everyone is trying to get their car sorted before the holidays start, so we're flat out with work and it's all hands on deck.' He tucked a broken pencil behind the larger of his protruding ears. 'Give us a buzz in the morning just to check, boss. But, assuming there are no major problems and the staff are not too hung-over, it should be ready by one o'clock.' He shook my hand firmly, grabbed his half-drunk mug of tea from the desk and strode purposefully to the ill-fitting door.

Outside in the bitterly cold air, I took out my phone to check for any messages. The only one was from Sandy; it read, 'It's country and western night at the Lion later.'

My heart sank as I was no fan of those theme nights. 'Are you having a laugh?' I texted.

'No. I thought it would be a nice change. If we don't like it we can go for a curry,' she replied.

'That's more like it. I'll see you shortly. Just dropped off the car.' I pressed the send button and slipped the mobile into my jeans pocket. I turned back towards Dave, who was smoking a cigarette while standing on the bottom step of the hut, and asked cheekily, 'Where's the courtesy car to take me home?'

'Whatever.' He smiled toothily while shaking his head vigorously and dismissed me by raising a right index finger like a cricket umpire.

The walk to the betting office, although short, was not quick. I was held up by a confusion of gossiping pensioners and elbowed my way through a gaggle of girls with their reproduction 1D jackets, fake Hello Kitty handbags and faded replica Ugg boots. Eventually reaching the shop, and anesthetised by the cold, I stepped into the warmth before recognising from behind two chancers, standing like a pair of constipated kippers as they carefully plotted their next betting coup.

I squeezed between the eternally optimistic dynamic duo and asked, 'All right, you two losers, what's happening?'

Shergar nearly swallowed the small plastic pen he was sucking as he turned in surprise. 'All right, dude, how's it hanging?' he asked.

'I'm OK, mate. Have you chosen any winners?' I asked pointlessly.

'No, I couldn't pick me nose. The last time I backed a winner Lord Nelson had just lost an eye.'

Biffo joined in. 'How's your luck, man?'

'Not very good. The last time I was successful, the old king was still alive,' I joked.

He chuckled. 'Join the club, man. If it wasn't for bad luck, I'd have no luck at all. We're all in the same boat, innit,' he said, trying to achieve the solidarity that groups of unsuccessful punters often seek. 'I see your little friend is behind the glass again.' Biffo tapped the side of his nose and winked knowingly.

'Oh, is she?' I asked and casually glanced over my shoulder.

Shergar peered towards the counter and said, 'Well, she was there. Perhaps she's gone on her break.'

I strolled to the only available window, where unsmiling Scottish Marjorie was serving, and passed across my slip. She scanned it and, without speaking or making eye contact, provided me with a receipt before I left the prison of possibilities where the hostages to fortune find it difficult to escape.

Outside I turned left and noticed that, less than ten

yards along the pavement, the object of my increasing obsession was waiting for me like Greyfriars Bobby. 'Hi, is it your break time?' I enquired.

'Yes, I needed a breath of fresh air. It's been hectic and I'm going to buy a can of pop at the newsagent's across the road.'

'Oh, I see. Are you serious about tonight?' I asked.

'Yes, why not? It'll be a good laugh.'

'I'd rather sandpaper my lugholes than listen to that type of music. And I'm not getting dressed up,' I objected.

'Nor am I.' She was trying to placate me. 'I'll just wear some jeans, boots and maybe a jacket.'

'That's OK, then,' I conceded reluctantly.

'We can see what it's like. We don't have to stay. Like I said before, we can go for a meal,' she said, still trying to persuade me.

'All right then,' I consented, deferring to her wishes and better judgment. 'Shall I meet you in the Lion because I'll have to walk?'

'Yes, that's fine. About 8.30.'

'Right, that's a date,' I confirmed with a cheesy grin. I glanced around swiftly then kissed her lightly on the mouth and squeezed her hand. A gentle breeze teased the dark brown fringe which framed her angelic face.

Later, in the warmth of my apartment and in a docile mood, I was vegetating in front of the afternoon sport. Bored almost to extinction, my mind focused on the forthcoming evening's entertainment. My mild protest to Sandy about the night out had fallen on deaf ears. I was not looking forward to it; I pictured the place full of overweight, middle-aged people in strange clothes, with massive silver-buckled belts. They'd be wearing funny hats and footwear they could barely stand up in, making fools of themselves as, choreographed by alcohol, they danced, pranced and stomped around and hollered, 'Yee-haw.'

I once read in a magazine that country music is about real issues, tears, pain and life's problems. Really? I think not; the songs are based on lying husbands, cheating wives, wild drinking, adultery, sin, lonesome highways, shooting, hanging, dead dogs and a horse that you can rely on. The argument that these songs are about truth and justice, and sung in a language that can be understood, is decimated by such titles as: 'You Must Be Over Me, 'cause Now You're Under Him', 'You're the Reason Our Children Are Ugly' and 'I Can't Believe You're Leaving but I've Packed Your Bags in Case'. Why had I been corralled into this cowboy carnival of chaos?

The pub was decorated in the style of an old Wild West saloon bar, with imitation horse brasses on the walls, wanted posters, pictures of gunslingers and a set of buffalo horns with a cowboy hat hanging between them. A male member of staff, decked out as John Wayne, served drinks, but anything he could do the female dressed as Annie Oakley could do better. They both wore tall Stetsons, boots with ornamental spurs and leather holsters belted around their waists, containing what I hoped were only replica guns.

When I ordered our beers from 'The Duke', I was greeted by, 'Howdy partner, what can I get you?' Thankfully the management had not tampered with the liquor by insisting that the clientele bought bourbon or moonshine.

We stayed for a tedious hour as the continuous whooping and hollering by the increasingly inebriated folks began to grate. The DJ forced us to listen to such legends as Johnny Cash, Tammy Wynette, John Denver and Willie Nelson but the tiresome jamboree was not quite our scene. Eventually we rang for a taxi and, ten minutes later, we were delivered from the Wild West back to civilisation.

When we arrived at the multi-award-winning Tear Drop of India on Manchester's famous Curry Mile, the temperature had dropped even further and a bitterly cold easterly wind prevailed. When we entered the warm and welcoming Sri Lankan restaurant, we were immediately surrounded by eager-to-please waiters; I imagined that their well-rehearsed manoeuvre was carefully designed to prevent any thought of escape. The infrastructure was stretched to breaking point as customers were shoe-horned into every available place except for a table for two at the rear, to which we were led.

Sitting opposite each other, I thought that Sandy seemed rather quiet and slightly withdrawn. Perhaps she was tired from working all day. 'Are you all right, babe?' I asked.

'Yes, I'm fine, thanks,' she replied, tossing her head back and brushing a loose strand of hair from her cheek. 'Why?'

'I just thought you seemed a little down. Have you been busy in the shop, or didn't you enjoy the Lion?'

'Work wasn't too bad but that shindig was rubbish and not my idea of fun.' She suppressed a yawn. 'I hoped it would be better than that but, heigh-ho, you live and learn.'

'No, it wasn't my thing either, but I did tell you this morning,' I gloated.

'All right, all right, we're here now. Let's have a nice

meal and forget about it.' She picked up the menu and studied it closely.

I lifted the wine list from its Perspex holder and asked, 'What would you like to drink?'

She inclined her head slightly and said, 'You choose. I don't mind. Don't stint. I know what you're like.' Then she stood up and marched away towards the ladies with her buzzing mobile phone.

As I looked at the wine selection, I reflected that she had been a little prickly for a few weeks. Like a lot of men faced with this scenario, the inevitable questions began to circulate in my mind. Had she gone off me? Had she found someone else? Was she still interested or was it all over? Was I trying too hard or going too fast? My seesawing emotions were driven away, however, when the starters arrived at our table.

After we had finished our food and a carafe of wine, I bravely raised the subject which had preoccupied me for several days. 'What are you doing for Christmas this year?'

'I don't know yet. Why?' she answered.

'I'm expected to go to my parents' house in South Yorkshire,' I revealed.

'Oh, that will be nice. You haven't seen them for six months or so, have you? You can catch up with everything.'

'That's right,' I agreed. 'But what are you going to do? I don't want to leave you on your own, especially at this time of year. Why don't you come to Sheffield with me?'

'Thanks, hon, but I've made plans. I've a mountain of course work to catch up on and I need to cram for the exams. Jessica is staying around for Christmas instead of going home to Brighton, so I won't be on my own.'

'Well, you are more than welcome to change your

81

mind. I've already asked my folks and they're cool about it. My mother said you can sleep in my room and I'll stay on the settee,' I said, grinning and still trying to persuade her.

'Thanks, but I'll be happy enough staying in Manchester. How long are you planning to be away for?' she asked.

'I'm not sure yet. Probably until the second of January. I have to be back at work on the fourth so I'll be away for the New Year as well.' I continued quickly, 'But I'll ring you every day. It's only a forty-minute drive so if you change your mind, I'll come and get you.'

'That's nice,' she beamed. 'Anyway, we'll see each other before Christmas, won't we?' she added a little uncertainly.

'Yes, definitely. I've got the office party to get through but, apart from that, I've nothing organised.'

'I've no doubt that you will want your present,' she remarked softly, fiddling coquettishly with her hair.

'Why, have you got me one?' I asked eagerly.

'Not yet.' She leaned forward, clasped my hand and dropped her voice. 'But I'm sure you'll want something to unwrap slowly, turn on and play with before Father Christmas comes.' She smiled seductively, licked her lips and flashed her crystal-blue eyes.

A short period of pouting and making promising smiles ensued before I ventured, 'Shall we go and have some fun, then?'

'Fun,' she echoed. She picked up her bag and said softly, 'Give me two minutes,' before heading down the corridor. Intrigued, I remained seated and brimming with anticipation until the smoke alarm unexpectedly burst into life. The excited staff directed the diners through the fire door as the sprinkler system began to dribble apologetically. Outside in the cold of the inadequately lit back yard, people scurried about anxiously in search of their friends.

I spotted Sandy's smirking features as she lurked in the shadows. She was stuffing a cigarette lighter into her handbag. I rushed across, we linked arms and scarpered into the darkness without paying the bill.

CHAPTER 9

Party Time

The approach of the Christmas break generated high excitement among the rank and file of the family-owned double glazing firm where I worked. This year the holiday appeared to coincide with the silly season as our customer service department was, apparently, waging war on both new and existing accounts. The 'sales prevention team' seemed hell bent on bickering over every minor detail of every contract, as well as adopting a totally inflexible attitude to the pricing policy for all potential new orders. The tried-and-tested maxim of 'the customer is always right' meant absolutely nothing to them; instead, they assumed the contrary stance of 'the customer is rarely, if ever, right'.

Worryingly, my own sales figures had taken a nosedive since the beginning of October and, as my commission was already low, I was starting to cast around for an alternative job. Since I'd joined four years earlier, the management, to their eternal credit, had only exerted mild pressure to encourage me to improve my efforts. But with the decrease in salary beginning to have a detrimental impact on my finances, the time spent travelling to and from work because of the traffic and the longer than industry standard length of my service, it was probably time for a change.

The sales director could often be found sitting in a shoebox-sized glass office, invariably with his glistening billiard ball of a head drooping in disappointment, with a piece of foolscap paper which spelt out an alphabetical list of employees' surnames resting sinisterly in front of him on a dark oak desk. The staff had labelled Clive with the dubious nickname of 'The Circumciser' due to his regular and disconcerting threats to make cuts all round. Aged in his early fifties and with a weather-beaten face, he had dullish blue eyes, a broad purple nose and crooked yellowing teeth. He was always turned out smartly, though, in a dapper suit with a freshly starched shirt and a loud tie. His body language, however, gave the impression that he was wearily carrying the weight of the world on his slim, sloping shoulders and I think the stresses and strains of the daily struggle at work, if not his home life, were beginning to grind him down.

Throughout my employment, our working relationship had been generally good, despite my refusal to join him in a round of golf at his lavish and exclusive Cheshire club which had only just voted in ladies and fizzy bottled water. I think he regarded me as a sensible individual who was capable of achieving targets and unlikely to cause any problems. I was not going to rock the boat or instigate trouble; in fact, I was perceived as a 'Steady Eddy' and he had often mentioned a possible promotion to team leader. In contrast, my colleagues were boisterous and unreliable. As sometimes happens in a competitive, male-dominated, high-pressure environment, the road can become bumpy. During my time there, I had witnessed fist fights, workplace bullying and bitter feuds caused by office romances; generally, however, my colleagues were as well-behaved as Japanese tourists.

It was surprising, given the scarcity of fresh enquiries in the third quarter, when Mr Botting announced to the assembled workers that, in keeping with tradition, there would again be a Christmas party at the Blue Bell Arms, situated conveniently across the road. The applause had hardly died down when he added, with a flourish of his arms and an ingratiating smile, that we would close an hour earlier in order to allow sufficient time for the employees to prepare for the fun and games.

Initially I was undecided whether to join in with the revelry. Eventually I decided that I would, not because of the various offers and promises whispered vaguely in my ear by some less choosy female members of staff, nor because of the unambiguous and shameless guarantee issued by Sophie from Swinton, but because of the irresistible allure of free food and drink.

Sometime later I was chilling on the sofa in my apartment with a cold can of beer, watching the regional news report on another motorway pile-up, the continuing bad weather and an infestation of mice in the grandstand at Rochdale Hornets. As the concerns of another frustrating and unproductive day ebbed away, my thoughts turned to the forthcoming function. I tapped out a text message to Sandy asking, 'Where are you, babe? Are you having a good day?'

I went to the window and watched the neighbourhood going rapidly downhill as daylight took its leave above the rooftops of suburbia. A small boy with ginger hair was playing keepy-uppy with a fluorescent orange plastic football in the gathering gloom across the road. Sad-faced office workers, buttoned up against a chill wind, scurried home for their tea, while next door's empty recycling bin was blown dangerously off the pavement.

I turned away and went into the bathroom before preparing for the evening. I wore a plain claret jumper, charcoal-grey trousers, smart black shoes and a modest dab of expensive cologne. I grabbed my heavy winter coat, hoisted up the collar and went out to the waiting cab, which delivered me to the welcoming arms of the Blue Bell.

The diners had finished dinner and the venue had been magically transformed into a traditional festive scene. Fragile paper chains hung delicately from the ceiling and mingled with animal-shaped balloons. A genuine pine Christmas tree stood tall and proud near the fire escape, dressed with glittering strands of tinsel and coloured baubles; a silver star shimmered on the top, while its multicoloured fairy lights twinkled in the semi-darkness. Freshly cut boughs of holly and ivy adorned the walls and there was a small sprig of mistletoe sited in a shadowy corner that I intended to avoid at all costs. Each table was covered by a thin white cloth depicting a variety of winter settings on which a small polystyrene Santa sat surveying the surroundings.

The evening was largely uneventful until I found myself trapped by an ebullient youngster with firework hair and chronic acne. He was tall, gawky and bespectacled and looked as pleased as a prince with a proper job.

The apprentice, obviously fancying his chances with the alcohol-infused ladies, had marinated himself in cheap aftershave, which made him smell like a tart's boudoir. He droned on tediously about subjects on which I had neither knowledge nor interest; eventually I escaped by tapping my empty glass with my right forefinger and glancing at my non-existent wristwatch. 'Good grief,' I said. 'Is that the time? I must go and get another drink.'

Near the end of the festivities, the company secretary suddenly capsized from her chair, asked for assistance from the Almighty and vomited violently into an expensive-looking handbag that belonged to the stern-faced finance director. The company secretary's spouse was summoned by phone before, fussing around like a mother hen, he whisked away the first casualty of the night.

In an effort to lighten the mood, I cracked a couple of jokes that went down like a broken lift. The remaining revellers were focused on downing copious amounts of booze at the company's expense; it was clear that they had no interest in holding a coherent or philosophical discussion.

For the next ten minutes or so I sat alone like a pork pie at a bar mitzvah until, having comfortably exceeded my limit, I decided to leave, despite spying sexy Sophie swaying seductively in a short silvery skirt with slinky silk stockings and strappy sparkly shoes.

A fanciful idea struck as I travelled home in the back of a lumbering and fume-belching old taxi. As full as a frog but with the courage of a lion, I impulsively decided to surprise my beloved by stopping at her flat for a goodnight kiss and cuddle. It is easy to convince yourself at the tender age of twenty-four that the euphoria of having a steady girlfriend will see you through to middle age and even easier to persuade yourself that, under the influence of a few pints, she will be delighted to see you.

Travelling through the dank streets, I reflected on the fact that she had never invited me to her place, which seemed strange, given the fact that she had stayed at my apartment on at least ten occasions. Cleaning and tidying is an act of betrayal in student accommodation but two girls sharing should be capable of maintaining a reasonable standard of cleanliness and tidiness. I was sure that the washing-up would not be neglected until the end of the week or the rubbish bins remain unemptied, which were features of my kitchen.

I ordered the cabbie to drop me off near the Golden Lion and walked to the suspicious-looking passageway that bisected the halls of residence. As I entered the dimly lit alleyway I noticed that it was stained by men who could not wait, and an overwhelming pungent stench attacked the back of my throat. My steps turned to strides, as though someone with a whip was chasing me.

I emerged breathlessly into a featureless, concrete square illuminated by a solitary lamp. A fine rain was falling and the moon was eclipsed by a thick blanket of cloud, which only enhanced the eerie atmosphere. After prowling around, as I was unsure which of the buildings to enter, I tossed a coin and plumped for the building above the door of which, in luminous orange lettering, read 'Poolborough House'.

I wrenched open the heavy door to the entrance lobby before spotting a yellowing notice telling me to lift the adjacent receiver and dial the relevant property flat. Unaware of Sandy's number, I made four unanswered attempts to locate her before a disgruntled man with an Irish accent rudely suggested that I try seventeen. This time, much to my relief, a sleepy female voice answered.

'Hello, is that Sandy?' I slurred hopefully.

A pause ensued before she muttered, 'No, who is it?'

'It's Mike, Sandy's friend,' I answered guardedly, swaying uneasily. 'Is that Jessica?'

'Yes, it is,' she confirmed peevishly. 'Sandy's gone out for the evening. I don't know what time she'll be back but I'll tell her you called round.' She added impatiently, 'Do you know what time it is?'

'All right, thanks for that. I'll send her a message,' I said, ignoring her question. Before I replaced the handset, the line went dead.

Retreating unsteadily from the foyer into the cold and wet night, I thought that it was a curious reaction from a young student at around midnight. They have a reputation, built up over many years, of getting off their faces and having it large in the many bars and clubs which service their needs until the early hours, rather than being tucked up cosily in bed. Perhaps Jessica was with someone, I speculated, before regaining some sense of reality and reminding myself that she was in her second year of studying law and therefore should be more sensible, responsible and grown-up than the rest of us mere mortals.

It was raining hard and deathly quiet as I made my way back home. Trudging along the deserted roads at midnight was not a habit to which I was accustomed. Only witches and cats walk in the dark, I thought, as I heard a dog howling slowly somewhere in the distance. It was the kind of scary scene that was reminiscent of an old horror film in which a bestial, homicidal maniac would abscond from a sanatorium on the moors. With these macabre thoughts in my mind, I was as jumpy as a kangaroo playing basketball on a trampoline as I hurried along the route. I struggled to navigate a plethora of puddles and uneven paving slabs, which cruelly shot jets of water into the air if you foolishly stood on the wrong part of them. My clothes were drenched and I cut a bedraggled figure but, in the absence of a passing car to offer me a lift, I kept going miserably.

A weird feeling of anxiety infiltrated the fuzziness of my brain. I was seized by painful doubt, as I could not recall Sandy saying that she was going out somewhere. Where had she gone? With whom? Why didn't she tell me? Why was she not home yet? In an attempt to banish these thoughts and achieve some peace of mind, I called her mobile but it was switched off. We had not been in touch all day, so where was she, I wondered with growing concern. Had we run our race? I sent a text in capital letters that simply asked 'WHERE ARE YOU?'

Keen to solve the mystery, I checked her Facebook for answers among the online community, where everyone seemed preoccupied with sharing everything, liking each other or poking one another, but there were no clues.

By the time I plodded into Primrose Avenue, sweating and steaming like a dray horse, with my spirits at rock bottom and resembling a drowned rat, she had still not responded.

Chapter 10

Not Going Out

The irritating din of a bell ringing in the distance invaded my dreams and woke me on the day before Christmas Eve. Slowly, wearily, I tried to gather my dulled senses, which had been severely impaired by the excesses of the annual office party held on the previous evening, as the realisation of the source of the disturbing racket began to dawn.

Struggling from the warmth of the bed and unsuccessfully searching through bloodshot eyes for my burgundy-coloured wine-bottle-shaped slippers, I hobbled stiffly across the room and wrestled my fraying dressing gown over my shoulders. I fumbled clumsily with the belt and moved dizzily like a tortoise on speed. Opening the door, a welcome sight stood blinking up at me in disbelief, shaking her head vigorously with disapproval. I must have looked ridiculous as I wobbled on legs of jelly in my undersized, beige towelling robe and bare feet. Sandy, however, appeared as fresh as a daisy with her springy dark hair, kissable cherry lips and a bright, clear complexion. In her left hand she clutched the handles of a yellow carrier bag, while a black canvas holdall was in the other.

'Good morning, lazybones,' she greeted me warmly, with a wisp of a smile.

'Good morning to you,' I croaked and yawned deeply while trying to adjust my vision to the bright daylight flooding in through the open doorway.

'Are you going to invite me in?' she asked, stepping forward.

'Of course,' I said. I shifted unsteadily to the side, allowing her to surge energetically over the threshold.

Feeling sweaty and light-headed as my memory began to unspool, I was still in a state of undress as we balanced side by side on the edge of the couch. Sandy patted my left knee consolingly and giggled at the absurdity of my self-inflicted predicament. 'Do you know what time it is?' she questioned.

I tried desperately to focus on the needle-like fingers that moved around the face of the brass clock that sat collecting dust on the corner shelf. 'Is that right? Five past twelve?' I went on and pointed shakily.

'Yes, near enough,' she answered. 'You don't look very well, hon.'

I groaned gently in an effort to garner some sympathy before placing one hand on my forehead and putting the other to my stomach. 'I feel as rough as sandpaper. And anyway, where were you last night? I rang, texted and even checked your Facebook page.'

Sitting bolt upright and glaring at me sternly, she replied, 'I told you last week that I was going out for a few drinks with some friends who are on my course.'

'I don't remember that,' I admitted, desperately scouring my memory bank.

'I did,' she insisted. 'You have the memory of a goldfish. It was last Saturday. You'd had quite a few beers and probably forgot – or you had your mind on something else,' she said defensively while scratching absent-mindedly at her ear.

'I can't recall. So why didn't you answer your phone?' I challenged.

'I forgot to take it with me. It was on charge and I left it in the flat. I got your voicemails and texts when I got home but it was too late to call. So I tried this morning but your phone is switched off.'

'Oh yeah,' I mumbled. 'I put it on silent after I called to see you. Did Jessica tell you?'

'Yes, she left me a scribbled note complaining that you had woken her up at some ungodly hour. What did you want?' She removed her hand.

'Nothing much,' I answered, a little embarrassed.

'Come on,' she encouraged and edged closer. 'What did you want, hon?'

'Well, I just wanted a little cuddle and a goodnight kiss, that's all,' I murmured shyly and glimpsing downwards.

'Oh, did you, Mike?' She thrust herself forward, throwing her arms around my neck and kissing me affectionately. 'Is that better?' she said, stroking my exposed lower thigh.

'I was getting really concerned and starting to panic. We hadn't spoken all day. Where were you?' I stopped her hand from progressing.

'I went shopping with the girls and had a Mexican

meal later.'

'What time did you get back?' I asked, still peeved.

'I'm not sure; about one,' she said vaguely.

'You should let me know in future,' I ordered.

'I did let you know. I told you last week but, like most men, you don't listen.'

'I don't recall,' I repeated.

'Well, I'm here now, safe and sound. That's all that matters,' she said, trying to pacify me. She stood up. 'Shall I make some brunch? Will it help with your hangover?'

I grinned like a Cheshire cat. 'That would be excellent if you're having some.'

'Have you got anything in the fridge?' she enquired.

'Yeah, yeah, it's all there.'

'Right, I'll crack on with that while you go and have a shower because you smell like a skunk,' she stated, hauling my fragile body upright.

As she went into the kitchen, singing, I spotted her baggage abandoned near the cupboard. 'What's in the bags?'

'Your pressies. I told you that I'd get you something. Have you got me anything?' she asked optimistically.

'Maybe,' I replied secretively. 'What's in the big one?'

'Just a few clothes,' she confessed. She walked back to me and nudged her leg between my unresisting knees. 'I know that you are going home tomorrow for the holidays, so we won't see one another for a fortnight and I thought that I would stay overnight, if you don't mind.'

I could not believe my ears as I absorbed her words and thought, 'Has Christmas come early?' I said, 'Certainly you can stay, you know that. It will be nice.'

'OK,' she agreed. 'I'll go and make something to eat.

You sort yourself out and take my things into the bedroom,' she instructed me like a bossy schoolteacher.

'No problem, miss, whatever you say. Your wish is my command,' and I heaved my sluggish carcass into action.

Later, we sat at the table eagerly tucking into bacon, sausage, dippy egg and brown toast, expertly prepared the way my mother used to make it when I was a youngster. The almost black, sugarless strong coffee instantly hit the spot. Sandy broke the silence by enquiring, 'Was your office party lit? Did you have a smooch with any of the girls or receive an offer from the slappers that you couldn't refuse?'

'Don't be silly. I had a drink, a bit of food and a chat with some colleagues. It was largely uneventful apart from the secretary throwing up violently into someone's handbag.'

She tossed back her head and laughed. 'No way. What happened next?'

'They sent for her husband and he rescued her,' I replied.

'So what time did you leave?'

'Shortly after eleven. I took a taxi to your place but when Jessica said you weren't in, I walked home.'

'What, in all that heavy rain?' Sandy looked incredulous.

'Yes. I was as wet as washhouse wallpaper and miserable as sin by the time I arrived here. There were no cabs, the streets were deserted and it was frightening. All sorts of things crossed my mind. I wondered what had happened to you, where you'd gone, why you hadn't told me. I was unsure whether you'd fallen out with me or if you didn't want to see me again.'

'Don't be ridiculous.' She reached across and clasped

my hand comfortingly between hers. 'That's not going to happen, is it?' she said earnestly.

'I hope not,' I replied.

'So do I.' She began to stroke my wrist reassuringly. 'You know that God made little donkeys and then, as though they weren't silly enough, he invented men as well.' I smiled broadly and clenched her fingertips so tightly that her polished red nails dug painfully into my flesh. 'You shouldn't be so insecure. Just because we're not in touch for a day or so, it doesn't mean that I have run away with someone or gone off you.'

'I know, but you could have texted or something,' I muttered and dropped my gaze.

'But I told you, without my phone how could I text?'

'You could have borrowed one from your friends,' I suggested but instantly realised the flaw in my logic.

'But I don't know your mobile number by heart. It's stored in my phone. So how could I ring or text?'

'Good point,' I conceded.

In an effort to calm matters, she skilfully changed tack. 'Why don't you go and chillax in front of the telly? I'll wash up and then we can vegetate in front of a good film.' She sounded like a doting wife.

Instead of protesting and offering to help, I went obediently and reclined luxuriously on the sofa. Lying flat on my back, with a still-throbbing head resting on a cushion, all the previous doubts and uncertainties vanished into thin air. While this heaven-sent angel of mercy was taking care of me in my hour of need, I could see through the window that the earlier brightness had given way to an angry-looking sky.

After she'd finished her domestic chores and slipped

off her shoes, Sandy joined me and lay down next to me. 'Are you feeling better now, hon?' she asked, while caressing my calf muscles.

'Yeah, I'm back on track,' I answered contentedly.

'Good, I'm glad. You're a brave little soldier,' she mocked. She relaxed and nodded off, while an old black and white film played quietly on the television.

Close to teatime I awoke from a short snooze and stretched lazily, as my companion pretended to be asleep. From her occasional eye movements, I could see that she was playing possum so, still top to tail, I started to tickle her foot. She giggled and her body writhed and squirmed as she begged for mercy but, holding her ankle firmly, I persisted.

'Get off,' she pleaded before finally kicking herself free. Like a cat, she sprang up and pounced on to me. We kissed tenderly as she spread her body over mine and my previous grouchiness subsided.

'I hope you're in a better mood now,' she whispered. The heady scent of her perfume coiled around my nostrils and her fringe brushed softly against my cheek.

'I feel a lot better. Do you?' I asked.

'I wasn't too bad. We didn't really overindulge,' she replied.

What do you say when words are not enough? I thought, as we lay tightly entwined for a couple of carefree minutes. I closed my eyes and experienced the feminine curves of her voluptuous body. The romantic moment was ended by her rumbling stomach. She lifted her glowing face from my chest and asked, 'What shall we do for tea?'

'Let's stay in,' I said. 'I just want to stay in this position for ever and ever.'

'I knew you'd say that,' she commented knowingly. During the past three months it seemed that we had built a strong bond and developed a mutual understanding, I thought, before she suggested that we might order a pizza.

After prising ourselves apart, we selected from a menu provided by mournful Maurice and his miserable mates who frequented the Bricklayers' Arms for a game of darts or dominoes. The meal deal was ordered and delivered within the hour by a middle-aged driver clad in a well-worn England football shirt, which reminded customers of the famous victory achieved on German soil in 2001. 'What's the score, boss, so to speak?' I asked.

'Eighteen quid, mate,' he replied toothlessly and handed over the order. I offered a twenty-pound note, rolled tightly like a cigarette. After he took the cash, we stood glaring like gunslingers, each daring the other to make the first move before he went for his pocket and reluctantly handed over the change. He retreated down the steps, triumphantly waving our free garlic bread.

'Where do you want it, babe?' I shouted in an effort to be heard above the music channel.

'I'll have it anywhere you want to give it to me,' she responded brazenly and followed me into the kitchen.

I turned, smirked and said, 'The pizza, I mean.'

'So did I,' she teased. 'Shall we be naughty and have it on our knees?'

'What, the food?' I queried cheekily.

'Hey, that's enough of that.' She jabbed me playfully in the chest with her index finger. 'I've brought something in a bottle, if you're interested.'

'What is it, a ship?' I joked.

She tutted and rolled her eyes like a disapproving nun.

'It's wine, lovely wine.'

'No, I'm off the alcohol today. I had sufficient yesterday. I'll have this lemon and lime that came with our order.'

'OK,' she said, before going spritely in search of the wine.

We attacked the takeaway and had almost finished when a sudden, spectacular bolt of lightning pierced the dark, followed immediately by a deafening clap of thunder which rocked the building to its very foundations. The storm had arrived with a vengeance and, as the rain drummed rhythmically on the windows, brilliant flashes lit up the inky black sky. As the deluge intensified and the rumbling increased overhead, we were shocked when, unexpectedly, the power failed. Our mobile phones provided the only source of illumination. I stood at the window and saw that the whole avenue had been plunged into darkness.

'Oh well, that's blown it,' I quipped and resigned myself to missing a movie which was scheduled for later.

'Don't worry, it'll be back on soon,' Sandy consoled me as she sipped thirstily at a large glass of red wine. Half an hour later, we were still in the dark. 'What shall we do now?' she asked, draining her drink.

'Shall we open our presents?'

'Come on, then.' I chased her into the bedroom and lit two candles, which had been purchased for such an occasion. I took down a gold-wrapped parcel from the top of the wardrobe and gave it to her, then watched spellbound as her expression changed as she enthusiastically tore open the flat box.

She shrieked with delight. 'Oh my God, it's fantastic! It's amazing, brilliant!' She embraced me affectionately. I'd bought the state-of-the-art silver laptop at the beginning of the month; it was both a bargain and a necessity for her ongoing studies.

'I thought you'd like it. You can use it for research,' I said, feeling extremely pleased with myself.

As she wiped away her tears, she kissed me passionately on the mouth and purred with delight. 'I'm so happy! I can't believe it. It's cool, it's awesome! It's just what I wanted. I've only got you a couple of little things, though,' she said, with a tinge of regret.

'Well, you know what they say: good things come in small packages,' I replied, trying to placate her. She rooted in her carrier and extracted two wrapped parcels. The first was a smart, blue, short-sleeved shirt and the second was an electric razor.

'Oh, tremendous! That's just what I need,' I enthused. 'Thanks, babe, they're fabulous.' I returned her kisses with interest.

Following the joyful exchange of gifts, we sat in the candlelight on the end of the king-sized bed. 'What shall we do next?' I beamed expectantly as she inched closer, held my hand and gazed at me.

'What would they do in the old days with no electricity, no radio and no TV? How did they amuse themselves?' she asked huskily, feigning innocence.

'I understand they used to make their own entertainment, so let's have an early night,' I suggested confidently.

'If you insist,' she conceded.

I reached for the white, heart-shaped top button on her frilly pink blouse, thinking that she really was the embodiment of a gift that keeps on giving.

CHAPTER 11

Old Acquaintances

The leaden sky was heavy with dumpling clouds and an early frost made the grass crackle when, just after lunchtime on Christmas Eve, I presented myself at my parents' house. I was desperately in need of a complete break from the stresses and strains of work.

Since flying the nest over four years ago, my bedroom had not been touched apart from the obligatory change of bedding, regular vacuuming and general airing. The life-sized posters of J-Lo and Anna Kournikova were still on the wall behind the bed headboard, flanking an enlarged photograph of the successful Manchester United team celebrating their memorable triumph in the 2008 Champion's League final. A pair of square-toed, brown leather shoes stood to attention in the bottom of the wardrobe from my last visit. Cecil, the stuffed cuddly tiger of my childhood, sat faithfully on a chest of drawers, observing the world through his one remaining plastic eye.

The evening passed quietly as we relaxed in front of the TV, watching tiresome reruns and seasonal specials which were being broadcast on all channels. Around nine o'clock my father rose from his favourite armchair, shook out his lethargy and announced, 'I'll get the bottle out.'

As sharp as a tack, my brother said cheekily, 'Not the rubbish stuff that tastes like it's straight from a catheter.'

My mother went into the kitchen and returned with a tray of freshly baked mince pies. After three full measures of the Special Reserve single malt whisky and two warm pastries, I retired to my bedroom without leaving either a reviving glass of sherry for Santa or even a crunchy carrot for Rudolph.

The following day dawned damp and dismal but, in spite of my advancing years, I skipped eagerly down the stairs like an expectant child. After getting on the outside of a full English, we gathered around the expertly dressed tree and handed out the presents. Noting the absence of a gift from Sandy, my mum innocently asked, 'Did your lady friend buy you a pressie, son?'

'Yes,' I replied guardedly. 'She gave it to me a couple of days ago.'

Somewhat mischievously, my dad joined in. 'Did you give her one?'

'I did at the same time,' I answered reluctantly.

My brother, trying to keep a straight face and suppress his laughter, pawed and played with his parcels.

Later, the Browns at number six came round, not only to spend some quality time with us but also to enjoy my mother's legendary roast dinner. They were in their fifties with no children and, from what I perceived, no excitement in their drab lives. Jean worked at the nearby dentist's; she was delicately built, with iron-grey hair, very timid and always appeared to be on the brink of tears. Mr B was employed by the Ministry of Incompetence, dowdy in appearance, uninteresting and seemingly afraid of his own shadow. We had nicknamed him 'Boring Bob'; we thought that he was the type of person who would never do anything risky, calculated or otherwise. It was no surprise that they had no offspring; I imagined that, during their thirty-year marriage, he had never plucked up the courage to ask his wife to remove her winceyette nightie before they hit the sack.

At noon, the three males were chomping at the bit and ready to walk the short distance to the Owl. Mrs B insisted that her downtrodden husband should put on his coat and join us on the annual pilgrimage. On entering the already vibrant venue, a Huggy Bear lookalike landlord observed the time-honoured custom of providing the first drink free of charge.

We managed to bag a smallish square table in the corner of the crowded saloon bar and sat surveying the other customers who were amusingly and unashamedly sporting an assortment of ill-fitting, unstylish, multi-coloured cardigans, jumpers and sweaters, evidently gifted by girlfriends, mothers and wives who ought to know better. Further along the gaffer-taped padded bench was an ashen-faced, charismatic septuagenarian, bent and crippled by rheumatism, affected by asthma and as deaf as a referee. Joe Shuttleworth was sitting alone in his usual place at his reserved spot and nursing a pint of mild in his dimpled, personal pot. For some time, the last-leg-looking old-timer watched me like a hawk as I absent-mindedly shredded a beer mat, before wheezing, 'Naa then, lad.

They tell me tha's gone living wi' t'enemy on t'other side of t'hill. Is that reet?'

'That's right, I moved to Manchester some time ago and have settled down there,' I replied respectfully.

'Dost like it? Cos theer funny buggers in Lancashire, tha knows,' he said with a twinkle in his eye.

'Yes, it's okay. I've got myself a nice apartment and a steady job,' I shouted.

'Hast got thissen a wench?' he probed before downing the dregs of his drink.

'I'm not sure about that. I'm interested in someone but it's early days.'

'Dost tha want any advice, cock?' he offered.

'Yes, go on, then.'

The old rascal smiled gummily, leaned forward and handed his empty glass to me. 'Put a drop in theer and I'll tell thee.' Without arguing, I went for his refill, bought a round and returned to our position under a wall-mounted loudspeaker.

'Here you are, Joe. Get that down your neck,' I said to the crafty old rogue.

'Champion. Ta, lad, tha's a good'un. Just remember what I tell thee. Dunner bother with women, they're nowt but trouble. Tha's better off keeping it in tha pocket.' He cackled and coughed and removed his dirty flat cap to reveal a hairless scalp criss-crossed with parched wrinkles. His infectious laughter spread like wildfire among the crowd – then suddenly he clutched his chest, blanched and keeled over. The sobering sound of the last orders' bell tolled and an ambulance was called.

At the end of the day, I turned in at around eleven o'clock. I was lonely and yearned for Sandy so I sent her a sloppy text in which I promised her the world, declared my undying love and wished she were here. However, sleep took over before she replied.

Boxing Day was bright, breezy and very mild for the time of year. My brother and I set off to watch Sheffield Wednesday weave their wizardry against their local rivals, Rotherham United. Navigating through the narrow streets of our home town, we were compelled to dodge in and out of the inconsiderately parked vehicles, while fighting off the recycling bins which, like Daleks, were evilly mobile and designed to cause the maximum impediment to human progress.

I watched a solitary redwing gorging on winter berries in the hedgerow, while a large grey goose lumbered into the sky, spewing entrails of exhaust above the English countryside. We approached Hillsborough Stadium armed with the two tickets that Kieran supposedly had won in a work's raffle that was so rigged that even Kim Jong-il would blush. I smelt the mouth-watering aroma of frying onions, grilling burgers and sizzling sausages, offered by a phalanx of takeaway vans outside the ground, before filing through the turnstile where a ruddy-faced, cheerful and helpful steward in a dayglo orange jacket guided us to our seats, well in time for the scheduled kick-off. I waited with enormous anticipation and great expectation for the start of the match, as the club's staunchest supporter had enthused throughout our journey that the home team had been 'playing some excellent football lately'.

Sitting among the parliament of Owls fans at the beginning of the game, a low winter sun shone like an angle poise lamp into my eyes until, having seen enough of the ill-tempered encounter, it wisely disappeared for the rest of the afternoon. Both defences, apparently still suffering with thick heads, kicked lumps out of anything that moved – and even those which didn't – in a frustrated effort to shake off their hangovers, while the normally tricky, elusive and skilful wingers played as though their boots were tied together. On one occasion our overrated striker, when clean through on goal, inexplicably and hilariously tripped over his own feet before going down in instalments, presumably affected by yesterday's over indulgences.

The shrill sound of the half-time whistle was met by hoots of derision and screeches of disapproval from the ruffled locals as we sagely swooped to the rear of the stand for a locally sourced pie and a pint. The soporific second half was no better, however, as the powder-puff, lightweight and impotent attacks failed to penetrate. At some point, I nodded off only to be roused by the grumbling spectators chanting 'what a load of rubbish' and boisterously braying for their brass to be returned. There is something rather comical about a tranche of tight-fisted tykes tearfully tilting at a refund, I mused, as we slipped silently away from the anticlimactic goalless draw.

The next afternoon, I decided to spend a few hours in the pleasant late-December sunshine looking for bargains in the local shops. As I contemplated the 50 per cent reduction on some smart-looking pinstriped trousers in the window of a menswear shop, I felt a gentle tap on my right elbow. I turned, to be faced by Lisa Battersby. With long golden hair, arctic-blue eyes, luscious lips and that unforgettable pair of massive attributes, I had not seen her since school and she appeared to have filled out since those innocent and naive times. 'I thought it was you,' she beamed broadly.

'Hi, it's nice to see you. How are you?' I responded cheerfully, and extended my right hand. To my surprise, she pushed it away, stepped forward and kissed me.

'Come on,' she said. 'We know each other better than that – or have you forgotten, big boy?'

Surprised, I rocked back on my heels and blushed like a teenager while recalling that old adage that 'you never forget your first time'. Although the magical moment is often brief, it stays in your heart forever.

'What are you doing these days?' I asked quickly.

'I settled down, got married and had this little one.' She glanced down at a silver pushchair which contained a small boy with brown eyes, chubby cheeks and an oversized yellow dummy protruding from his mouth.

'Very good,' I said, stooping to get a closer look. 'What's his name?'

'He's called Steven.' She smiled maternally. 'My other half chose it. It's his middle name. Anyway, how are you doing? I bumped into your kid some weeks ago and he mentioned you'd gone up in the world. Said you were running your own firm, bought a house and are getting engaged.'

'Not quite,' I scoffed. 'I work for a glazing company, I have an apartment and I've just started seeing someone. What about yourself?'

'After failing my exams, I worked in a soul-destroying call centre for five years, got hitched and I spend my time now bringing up this toddler.' She bent down, kissed the baby and straightened again. 'What are you doing back home?'

'Nothing much. I just came for Christmas to see my

folks and I needed some fresh air,' I replied.

'Well, I'm going for a livener in the Jockey. It's happy hour soon, so come in with me,' she suggested.

'No, no,' I protested.

'Go on,' she said. 'It's a good laugh in there. Some of the old gang go in. My hubby is on lates so you can keep me company. I'll look after you,' she urged.

'I better not. I'm expected back by five; my tea will be ready,' I declined weakly.

'It's up to you, but if you change your mind you know where I am.' She grabbed the handles of the buggy and wheeled it away, wiggling her bottom provocatively. Open-mouthed, I gazed wistfully after her. When she stopped to wave, the gentle breeze tugged at her ringlets before she turned the corner and was gone.

The rest of the week dawdled peacefully by without incident until New Year's Eve. Due to the anticipated numbers expected to join in the revelry, the Owl's proprietor decided that the doors would be closed from eight o'clock and anyone who failed to meet the deadline would be refused admission. With this in mind, Kieran and I arrived with ten minutes to spare. After shoving past the men in short sleeves and superfluous dark shades, we barrelled through until we were compelled to share a table near the dart board with a couple of regulars. They were slumped drunkenly round a box of dominoes.

As we joined them, Dixie said, 'Here he is, Woodhouse's answer to Richard Branston. He'll get us all out of the pickle. They tell me you're single-handedly running Manchester's business community.' He gave a raucous laugh and eyed his companion for support.

'Yes,' concurred Whopper, adjusting his glasses. 'We've

been told you're the northern powerhouse.' He guffawed and pounded his fist against his thigh. 'You bright sparks are all the same,' he said, alluding to my brother's profession.

'Leave him alone,' Kieran interrupted. 'He's as thick as the rest of us.'

'He's not as bad as you,' said Dixie after a slight hesitation. 'I remember when you had an allergic reaction to a mushroom facial scrub you bought from the beauty shop cos you thought it was pâté.' He arched back, throwing his hands to the heavens and roaring uncontrollably, while the cologne-soaked sycophants within earshot joined in his delight.

'Yeah, yeah, yeah,' responded our kid. 'I've heard it all before. It wasn't funny then and it isn't now. You need some different material. Are we having a game of bones or what?'

After the hilarity dissipated, we wasted some time playing a few games until we gave up through boredom.

An hour later, a brace of very brave or extremely foolish females ventured into the male bastion of the taproom. They perched on high bar stools while rhythmically swinging their legs in time to the music which was pulsating from the sound system. The larger of the women kept eyeing me as though trying to recall my name. She seemed vaguely familiar as she rocked unsteadily in her strappy peach dress. She had long chestnut hair and a tattoo of a serpent slithering from her right shoulder down her back to who knows where.

We looked at one another for several moments until, on my way to the gents, I realised that it was an old classmate. 'Hi, are you Jane Middleton?' I asked.

A flicker of recognition spread across her plump face. 'Is it Mike Carpenter?' she slurred uncertainly.

'It is,' I confirmed and offered my hand.

'How are you? I've not seen you for ages,' she squealed weightily before hopping down from her stool. 'I thought it was you but I wasn't sure. It's nice to see you again.' She smiled widely.

'And you,' I said in return. 'I don't live in these parts any longer, so you won't see me knocking about.'

'Oh yes, that's right.' She tapped the side of her head. 'Someone told me you were working abroad, you were a big success and you've done really well for yourself.'

'That's stretching the point a little,' I replied dismissively, while thinking that gossip is like a forest fire: hard to extinguish. 'What about you? How are you doing?'

'Yes, I am good,' she answered unconvincingly and shook her mass of hair. 'I'm married with two children, a boy and a girl.'

'Excellent. Are you working?'

'What, with a couple of kids and a house to run? I just stay at home, bring them up and wait on my lazy, shiftless partner,' she said gloomily and sipped her drink.

'I see. It's like that, is it?'

'Unfortunately so. He was in our year. Do you remember Tommy Sutcliffe?'

Her words sliced open old scars. A cold chill went up my spine and my heart sank as I recalled Torturing Tom, that seeping wound of malevolent pus. He had a violent and ungovernable temper and was the school bully. He strutted about, well-insulated by his own stupidity, and used to shove my head down the toilet, flush it and call it a swirly. He used to bend back my thumbs and beat me up for my snack money until I told my elder brother, who went around to his house and dished out a good kicking. Strangely, after that he never spoke to or came near me again.

'Of course I remember him. How's he doing?' I asked, not really giving a damn.

'He's currently out of work. He got sacked six months ago for stealing from the megastore, so he just gets under my feet all day,' Jane complained and bowed her head in shame.

'No way,' I exclaimed.

'He's always been like that. He can't keep his hands to himself, the silly sod,' she concluded sadly.

'Anyway,' I said, shifting from one foot to the other, 'it's been nice catching up with you. Take care of yourself.' I squeezed her fleshy hand and hurried away to the toilets.

On the stroke of midnight, the turn of the year was ushered into the strains of 'Auld Lang Syne'. The windows and doors were flung open to allow clear air and fresh hope to circulate. The customary exchange of high-fives and well-wishing ensued as the drinkers from the lounge mingled with those from the spit-and-sawdust.

Jane came back into our side of the pub and made a beeline for me before planting a smacker on my mouth with her freshly glossed lips and wishing me all the best. I instinctively reciprocated.

'Why don't you give me a buzz sometime?' she asked. 'If you're staying in the neighbourhood for a few days, I can arrange a babysitter and we can spend some time together.' She winked.

Peering through beer goggles, I considered her offer seriously before regaining my senses and saying, 'I'd love to but sadly I'm going home the day after tomorrow. Perhaps next time I am in the area,' I added, trying to let her down gently.

I looked up. Standing directly behind her was the unmistakable, imposing figure of her partner. His massively strong hand reached over and clamped tightly onto my bicep. With hairs springing from his flaring nostrils and a burger-sized purple bruise beneath his left eye, he demanded menacingly, 'How long you in town for, Carpenter?'

'I'm going back in a day or so,' I blurted out, as he dug in his thumb and the searing pain intensified.

'Good. Don't hurry back, will you?' he said threateningly.

'I won't,' I agreed feebly, trying to wriggle free. 'But Kieran still lives here. Do you remember him from our school days? He'll help you if you need anything.' My courage was renewed as my bulky brother swaggered into view. Sutcliffe released his hold immediately as my saviour bore down on him and the room fell silent.

'You're in the wrong bar, pal. Get back in the other side. You're out of your depth, if you get my drift,' Kieran snarled.

As most bullies do when someone stands up to them, Sutcliffe backed down and retreated, dragging his unfulfilled spouse behind him. A spontaneous round of applause broke out before I unsuccessfully attempted to ring Sandy in order to wish her all the best.

CHAPTER 12

Meet the Folks

Although raw, it was a bright and dry mid morning on the first Sunday in February when we set off to have lunch at the three-bedroomed, semi-detached family home in South Yorkshire. The latest in a long line of invitations had been issued at the beginning of the week and, unlike the previous requests, I had accepted gratefully. The level of anticipation rose when Sandy surprisingly agreed to accompany me; my previous attempts at persuasion had been graciously but firmly declined.

In order to pick up Sandy, I stopped in the car park of the Golden Lion. The ruddy-faced landlord was standing at the side of the entrance. Wrapped in a muffler and thick winter coat, he puffed languidly on a cherrywood pipe, sending up lazy smoke while watching admiringly as his teenage nephew disinfected, scraped and swept away the devastation caused by last night's hammered revellers.

Wreathed in smiles, Sandy manoeuvred herself into

the warmth of the car. She was wearing a pretty salmon-pink scarf folded neatly into the top of her black jacket and a sexy blue denim skirt. Her short dark hair had recently been washed and her make-up, it seemed, had been painstakingly applied.

'You look fabulous,' I complimented her, but received only a cursory shrug of the shoulders in response.

The car snorted sullenly when we drew away and headed eastwards into a low, blinding winter sun. Listening to the music playing on the radio, my passenger appeared lost in thought as she gazed through the window at the bleakness outside. Her hands rested delicately in her lap, her thin fingers interlocked. It was not until we started downhill to the icy landscape of Yorkshire that she asked, 'How long is the journey?'

'About forty minutes,' I replied, squinting as the sunshine reflected off the surrounding frost.

'That's the length of time it takes to put a girdle around the centre of the earth,' she said, making an obscure literary reference to a speech delivered by Puck in *A Midsummer Night's Dream*. I nodded, not really listening but preferring to concentrate on driving safely in the treacherous conditions. 'I've never been to Sheffield. What's it like?' she asked.

Taking my time, I began. 'When I was growing up, it always seemed to be a cheerless city, depressing and miserable. If you walk up and down the same street twice, you've seen them all. Everywhere and everything is grey and dreary, especially at this time of the year. But it's a very historic place, which was built on a world-famous steel industry and used to be dependent on the nearby working coal fields. Sadly that sector has largely closed down and

Sheffield has been forced to innovate and modernise. A lot of the people here look miserable most of the time. I think they've given up hope and have just stopped trying. When the female population are on a night out, they hunt in packs for their unsuspecting prey. They are some of the ugliest munters in the county and they should be wearing bells around their necks. There's a blotchy road sign near to where I lived that reads "Only thirty-eight miles to Manchester". Somebody's written underneath "Thank the Lord for that. There is still hope".'

'Great. It sounds lovely. You paint a very appealing picture. I'm looking forward to it immensely,' Sandy responded sarcastically, lowering her window fractionally as we pressed on.

Approximately a mile from our destination, we swung sharply right into Vicarage Avenue and continued along a road lined with bare trees, now bent and gnarled by age. Sandy correctly observed that there was, in fact, no vicarage.

'You're dead right,' I confirmed. 'There is actually a story behind that.'

'Go on,' she encouraged me before settling back into her seat.

'Well,' I started, 'about ten years ago, a baby-faced, down-with-the-kids fifty-year-old vicar was accused of embezzling sixty grand from the church funds. Nobody could believe that he would do a scandalous thing like that – but then he eloped with the already-married local postmistress. She was only in her late twenties, very attractive and with a reputation for promiscuity.'

'What happened next?' Sandy asked with growing fascination.

I don't know. Neither she nor the immature and disgraced Peter Pan of the Pulpit, who used to put the world to rights and the fun into funerals, were ever heard of again. Four years ago, the place was torched by vandals before the council demolished the remains for safety reasons, as you can clearly see.' I gestured towards the derelict site before continuing along the road until, under a bruised purple sky, we turned into Church Lane.

Number twenty-six had been our family home for almost three decades, since my parents moved there from Altrincham following their marriage in 1985. Arm in arm, Sandy and I slid along the path that bisected the garden. In warmer times, it was lush with fuschia, skimmia and roses but today the chill wind tweaked the linings of our lungs and ran its icy fingernails up our nostrils. The neatness of the garden was attributable to my mother, whose hobby, if not obsession, was to maintain it to a very high standard.

Lightly pressing on the star-shaped bell, I felt Sandy squeeze my arm tightly against her ribs, seeking reassurance. A few seconds later the red door swung inwards and a wave of warm air hurtled out. My mother beckoned us across the threshold and embraced me quickly, then flung her arms theatrically around Sandy, smiling with delight and affectionately patting her on the shoulder. My father adopted a more measured approach, firstly shaking me by the hand enthusiastically and then offering a strong paw to Sandy. 'How do, luv. It's nice to meet you. Come on through and get warm.'

'I'm fine, thank you,' Sandy replied politely. 'We appreciate the invitation.'

The kitchen was situated immediately to the left of the hallway. A mouth-watering aroma of meat cooking slowly in the oven wafted through. In our close-knit circle, my mum's traditional roast beef and Yorkshire pudding, with all the trimmings, were legendary. A round, mahogany table with a highly polished top stood expectantly in the dining area adorned by condiments, cutlery and place mats.

We took off our jackets and were ushered into the lounge at the rear of the building. From the lemon-fresh aroma that permeated the room it appeared that, acting on orders issued before our arrival, my dad had vacuumed the floor, waxed the sideboard and dusted the ornaments. At first we sat awkwardly at either end of the three-seater sofa, not daring to move because of the exact arrangement of the plump cushions. A few minutes elapsed before my father broke the deafening silence. 'Who wants a drink?' he asked.

'I'll have a pint of Yorkshire's best as I'm in these parts,' I said, trying to curry favour.

He nodded and asked, 'Do you want to try my home-made elderberry wine, young lady?'

'Yes, please, but just a small one,' Sandy said, without dropping her smile. My father rose and left the room. Sandy crabbed along the sofa, placed her hand in mine, squeezed it and kissed me passionately.

'You'll ruin your lipstick,' I protested weakly.

'I don't care,' she said and did it again.

At that moment, I felt as happy as a child who had successfully persuaded his friends to come to his birthday party. She leaned across me, took a chocolate from a glass bowl on the coffee table, bit it and popped the other half into my mouth. Giggling, she placed the tip of her nose against mine and stared deeply into my eyes as if trying to see right into my soul and read my thoughts. That wouldn't have been hard to do as she had placed her hand a little too high on my right thigh.

The temptress shuffled back and resumed her original position when my father returned and handed out the drinks. Not long afterwards we heard the thunder of heavy footsteps as my brother rapidly descended the stairs. Sandy seemed startled when Kieran bulldozed his way in and grunted, 'All right, our kid?' He flopped down onto the only available seat and started to put on his shoes.

'Hello,' we both replied.

'I'm going down the Owl for a session with Dixie and Whopper. Do you want to come?' he asked, staring directly at me and avoiding eye contact with Sandy.

Dixie and Whopper, I mused, Woodhouse's answer to Morecambe and Wise. Barry Dean was nicknamed after the prolific pre-World War Two footballer, Dixie Dean; Darren Lyons was labelled Whopper not only because of his vastly overweight physique but also his addiction to Burger King.

I declined Kieran's offer. Without saying anything more to anyone, he jumped to his feet, stormed from the room and departed for the pub. This act of rudeness prompted my mother to come bustling in from preparing the meal with a red face, her stained apron flapping and clutching a flour-covered rolling pin.

'That lad worries me,' she declared, frustration in her voice. 'I don't know what's wrong with him these days. He seems troubled by something. Why can't he find a nice young girl, settle down and get married?' she said, wielding the wooden weapon like a conductor of a symphony orchestra. Then unexpectedly, and wide of the target, she added, 'That's probably what you pair have come to tell us. Or is there some other piece of good news?'

Chapter 13

Promises, Promises

After leaping energetically out of bed and bounding purposefully to the half-opened window, I discovered that February the fourteenth had dawned perishingly cold and very snowy. A thick white quilt smothered the surrounding area, stretching as far as the eye could see and muffling the roar of heavy traffic which rumbled and honked its way through the rush hour.

I gulped in the bracing air while watching a tiny brown shih tzu fearlessly hurtle head first into a mound of powdery snow before somersaulting several times, rolling on his back and furiously waggling his spindly paws. Suddenly changing his mind, he regained his feet, shook his quivering body and scurried back inside number twenty-three with his tail between his legs.

Further along the avenue, a large, thickset man started a snowball fight with his two small sons until, breathless, red-faced and frozen, they changed tack and began to build a snowman. On the doorstep a woman wrapped in a maroon dressing gown and wearing slippers smiled maternally at her children until, chilled to the bone and on the brink of tears, she waved them in.

Turning away from the wintry scene and this spectacle of domestic bliss, I recalled my own childhood when our father would take my brother and I sledging on Coopers Hill. We used to skate on the ice-covered duck pond and walk through the frozen woods, as the freezing temperatures nipped our noses, fingers and toes.

I remembered vividly that on one occasion my accident-prone brother tumbled from a home-made toboggan before rolling down the slippery slope until he collided with a tree that unsurprisingly dislocated his left shoulder. He was taken to the nearby hospital where my dad was forced to wait with him for so long that he missed a corporate afternoon at the football, while I stayed cosily at home, drinking hot chocolate and sampling my mum's freshly baked cookies and coconut macaroons.

I came back to the present when my mobile rang. Snatching it from the inside pocket of my leather bomber jacket that hung limply behind the door, I pressed the answer button and ordered, 'Speak to me.'

'Hi, there. Happy Valentine's Day, darling,' Sandy greeted me.

'Happy Valentine's Day, darling,' I repeated silently. 'Did she just call me darling?' During the five months that we had been going out together, she had never used that kind of language; in fact, she had avoided any kind of endearment.

'Happy Valentine's Day to you. Did you receive the bouquet I sent?' I asked. I was in danger of giving men a good name.

'Oh yes! The flowers are stunning. How did you know they are my favourites?'

'Just a lucky guess,' I said glibly. 'Most women like flowers, don't they?'

Earlier that week I had ordered a dozen long-stemmed sunset-red roses, embellished by a yellow satin ribbon, from the Forget-Me-Not flower shop near where I worked. The owner, Samantha, had worked as a receptionist in our office but I vaguely recollected that there was some sort of a scandal with one of the directors and she left under a cloud to set up her own business. She helped me pick a spray of flowers and guaranteed that they would be delivered on the right day and to the correct address.

I was a little stuck for words, however, when she asked, 'What do you want to say on the message card?'

Nervously fidgeting from one foot to the other, and with a degree of desperation, I asked, 'What do men normally write?'

She shrugged impatiently and said unhelpfully, 'Oh, lots of different things. It's up to you.'

'Right.' With a degree of embarrassment, I dictated a sloppy message. Sandy had obviously taken the sentiment to heart as she promised to show her gratitude later that evening by singling me out for special treatment. We arranged to meet at the restaurant in which we had enjoyed our first meal together.

Later, the snows retreated and driving was less hazardous as I made my way to Altrincham to visit my paternal grandmother. Trips of this nature were both infrequent and short; Granny Joan always seemed preoccupied with scolding me for having neither a proper job nor being in a steady relationship. She had lived alone in sheltered accommodation for more than seven years since the sad and untimely passing of Grandpa John. She was about five feet tall, slim, with ghostly coloured hair and sparkling blue eyes; her skin was so thin it was almost luminous. Despite being slightly arthritic and displaying a high degree of forgetfulness, she remained alert, cheerful and enthusiastic. She was more than willing to offer her opinion on any subject and she was never wrong. However, she could be argumentative and aggravating.

'Are you still selling windows and conservatories?' she snapped accusingly.

'Yes,' I replied sheepishly, as I knew what would follow.

'A salesman is not a solicitor,' she asserted.

'No, I can't argue with you there,' I yielded.

'Nor is he an accountant, doctor or part of any of the established professions. Why don't you get yourself a proper job?'

'Times have changed,' I replied defensively. 'The old expectations and values that you grew up with are no longer valid.'

But the old lady was not beaten yet. 'Do you get a lot of trouble with people taking drugs in the sales world?' she asked provocatively. 'Because I'm fully aware that drugs are an occupational hazard in your stressful line of business.' I did not reply. She persevered. 'I hear lots of people stick heroin up their noses.'

'That's cocaine,' I corrected.

Undeterred, she waded on. 'I suppose all the cheap young tarty girls throw themselves at you all the time.'

'They haven't done so yet,' I replied. 'Anyway, what do you know about it?'

Her brow furrowed and her eyes narrowed. 'I'm not an old stick-in-the-mud,' she said indignantly. 'Nowadays young women smoke in the streets, they go into pubs unaccompanied and I know that they have premarital sex. I do hope that you don't meet a girl like that!'

'No,' I replied, exasperated. 'I'm very sensible and determined to mature fully as a person before I tie myself down. Anyway, I think your view of modern life is out of bloody date!'

'No it's not,' she protested. 'I'm with it, yeah! I really know where it's at, innit. And stop swearing; it's neither big nor clever.'

'Sometimes,' I said, with increasing frustration, 'particularly when talking to you, I have a very strong desire to swear a lot.' I stormed out, leaving the acerbic old-timer on her own.

On the short car journey to my next rendezvous, I reflected on the emotionally bruising battle which had just taken place. When and why had this white-haired witch who, according to family gossip, used to have an optimistic outlook on life and single-handedly helped to keep Britain's pecker up after the Second World War, become so confrontational? Granted, she had always been belligerent, but in the past you could have a reasoned and well-thought-out discussion with her. In my view, this latest exchange had been a downright personal attack on her youngest grandson. It might be due in part to the high blood pressure, poor diet and the ravages of time that had hastened the onset of dementia and caused her aggressive behaviour. But it was still upsetting.

After the thirty-minute session of verbal jousting and a spiritually crushing experience with Granny Joan,

I was in desperate need of sympathy. My date was already waiting outside Guiseppe's Trattoria, snuggled against a knife-edged northerly wind in a fur-lined jacket with the hem of her pale blue dress showing just below her knees.

'Thanks for the fabulous flowers, hon. They were perfect,' she said, before we embraced affectionately.

'No problem. I'm glad you like them,' I replied.

'Yes, they're fab. The only thing is, I suppose I'll have to spend the next seven days flat on my back with my legs in the air,' she said saucily.

'Why, haven't you got a vase?' I replied cheekily.

She poked me hard in the middle of my chest with her index finger. Leaning forward, she whispered, 'I'll have you for that, really have you.' Then she kissed me passionately. Very much at ease with each other, we went into the restaurant.

A softly spoken waiter guided us to our seats, where a candle flickered in the centre of the table for two. The flame danced magically, casting its spell. The small restaurant was crowded with love-struck couples.

After slipping off her jacket and sitting down opposite me on a red velvet seat, I noticed that Sandy's elegant dress featured a very deep, plunging neckline. She had a small, silver heart-shaped brooch above her left breast. It was then that I finally realised: she was gorgeous, bright and mesmerising. For the first time in my life, I was in love.

We were holding hands loosely across the crisp white tablecloth while flirting and playing footsie underneath when the waiter reappeared with a pad and pencil at the ready to take our order. Sandy looked at the menu in silence before ordering for us both. Her choices were perfect: sautéed mushrooms topped with Dolcelatte cheese to start, followed by tagliatelle bolognese and, for dessert, individual tartlets filled with sour cherry jam and almond custard. The wine was good and she noticeably relaxed as she neared the end of her first glass.

After we finished our second bottle, we prepared to leave. Having done full justice to the meal and feeling deliriously happy, I rose and moved a little unsteadily to the other side of the table to help with her jacket. Taking my time, I started to fasten the three ruby-coloured buttons and paused momentarily when I reached the top.

'You,' she whispered feigning disapproval. 'I know what you're doing.' She leaned forward and gave me a passionate kiss then guided my hand onto her firm bottom. She continued, 'On this night of all nights, when lovers' dreams come true, I'm going to fulfil your every wish.'

I settled the bill and Sandy left a five-pound tip from a tight bundle of notes, then we scurried outside into the clear and crisp night and clambered excitedly into the back of a waiting taxi.

CHAPTER 14

Moving Day

Although that first Sunday in March was not memorable to most people, I'll always remember it because it was the day that Sandy moved into my humble apartment.

Clambering stiffly from the warmth of my bed after slightly oversleeping on that momentous morning, I ran into the kitchen and quickly flicked on the central heating before rushing back to the bedroom to get dressed. For a while I sat apprehensively on the edge of the bed considering the advantages and disadvantages of cohabiting with a sensible and practical young woman. I was expecting good company, stimulating conversation and unrestrained intimacy, along with splitting the bills, sharing the mortgage and dividing the domestic duties. At the same time, I would no doubt be forced to suffer never-ending episodes of *EastEnders*, lengthy occupation of the bathroom and Sandy taking over most of the available storage space for her various outfits, collection of handbags and multitude of footwear. However, if I played my cards right, my meals would be cooked, shirts ironed and there would be someone to snuggle up with on the cold and long nights. In return, I would need to become more patient and tolerant.

There are many good things about being single but they become inconsequential when you start a new relationship and decide to set up home together, I mused, after completing the tidying up.

The ringing of my phone jolted me back to the present. 'Hi, hon,' Sandy's sweet voice greeted me down a crackly line.

'Hello to you,' I replied. Was she calling to tell me that she had changed her mind about relocating?

'Are you okay? All set and ready for me?' she asked excitedly.

'Yes, everything is shipshape. I've vacuumed all of the rooms and cleared some space for your things,' I replied.

'Well done. We're just about to load the vehicle and leave, so I should be there in half an hour or so.'

'No problem. I'm not going out so I'll be ready and waiting for you.' I hesitated slightly before seeking reassurance. 'Do you think we'll be all right? As a couple, I mean. Can we make it work and be happy with each other?'

'Of course we can. We must. It's what we want and I'm determined to make it happen.' Her voice changed and I could hear her concern. 'Why? Have you got cold feet? Are you having second thoughts?'

'No, it's nothing specific. It's what we discussed and planned but I've never lived with anyone before. I'm unsure what to expect from this kind of commitment.'

'Apart from living here for the past eighteen months with Jessica, I've never shared with another person, let alone a man. It will take me time to get used to you and learn your habits and idiosyncrasies. But it will be a partnership, a two-way street. I'm slightly nervous too, and a bit frightened about what the future might hold, but I'm determined to give it a go.'

'I'm just seeking some moral support. Ignore me, take no notice. I'm ready and willing to take the next step with you,' I responded.

'Look, I'll be there shortly. We can have a chat and take it from there,' she promised calmly. She blew me a kiss and hung up.

I remained standing at the window for a few seconds, contemplating the forthcoming life-changing events. I stared out at the dismal weather then, gathering myself up, I started to polish vigorously at the teacup rings that stained the dark oak sideboard.

Winter was on the verge of giving way to spring the day Sandy moved into my tidy and aired bachelor pad. The sky was gunmetal grey and cheerless, with an East Manchester mizzle stubbornly refusing to clear. I was sure that if these climatic conditions prevailed during the cricket season, the players would be forced from the field and would return to the sanctuary of the pavilion, citing either bad light or rain stopped play.

A 'man with a van', together with his assistant, arrived just before coffee time. They were accompanied by my Sandy and her modest assortment of bags, boxes and cases. The younger of two men was blonde-haired, clean-shaven and very muscular; he had a tattoo across the knuckles of his right hand which stated, rather antagonistically, 'I hate City'. The taller and older of the two was fatter, bald as a coot and heavily bearded. He also displayed some artwork on his skin, which proclaimed 'I am the one and only'. He spoke with a thick, dreary Birmingham accent and irritatingly persisted in referring to Sandy as 'Cupcake'. They whistled tunelessly and swore shamefully as they pressed on.

As there was not a lot of heavy lifting or fetching and carrying required, the job was completed in double quick time. Afterwards, the four of us sat crammed in the kitchen slurping scalding instant coffee from chipped mugs and crunching broken biscuits. We swapped idle banter, while sitting around the wooden table.

The two men smelt of last night's booze, stale fags and chronic body odour. The City-hating man enquired, 'How long have you two been together?'

'About six months,' I replied, resenting his interest.

'So you thought you'd take the plunge and move in together?' he asked.

'Yes, we thought we'd give it a go.'

'You'll be fine,' he insisted, touching my shoulder reassuringly. 'She is a lovely girl. You've done well for yourself. Don't blow it,' he added, before winking sleazily. Then he started picking at his discoloured teeth and wiped his nose on the back of his hand.

The other man drained his mug, pushed back his chair and stood up. 'It's time we got going. Is everything OK, mate?' he asked before thrusting out his hairy right arm and offering his greasy palm. Unwillingly, I fished around in the pocket of my jeans and pulled out my last tenner before slapping it begrudgingly into his sweaty paw.

'Yes, it's fine,' I conceded, while at the same time berating myself for tipping people who are only doing their job.

When they had mercifully departed, I closed the door and immediately went around flinging open all the windows. Although the noon air was bracing, the suffocating stench left behind by the gruesome twosome was turning my stomach and making me dry retch.

'What's the matter?' asked Sandy, noticing my screwed-up face.

'It's them. They stank of BO,' I explained. My father's words echoed in my mind: 'It's the smell of good honest graft.'

'Yes, they were a bit ripe,' she conceded. She grabbed the green can of air freshener from the shelf in the corner and began to spray the alpine-fresh fragrance liberally in each room.

When the Sunday afternoon omnibus edition of a popular soap, with its wildly improbable 'jumping the shark' storylines, had mercifully ended, we went into the bedroom to complete the unpacking. We hadn't spoken a single word about our telephone talk earlier that day.

The oversized duvet was neatly arranged and on the left pillow crouched a soft toy tiger. 'Who's that?' Sandy shrieked with horror and pointed accusingly.

'It's Cecil. I've had him since I was a boy,' I explained. The stuffed tiger with its orange and black stripes was given to me as a present for my second birthday. Sadly, he was showing distinct signs of ageing and general wear and tear: his fur was patchy, his tail frayed and he exuded a rather strange, musty smell. Only one bluish plastic eye remained; the other had been lost in a brutal and prolonged battle with the family dog, Rex, shortly after my sixth birthday. Half of Cecil's left ear was missing and a two-inch scar on the back of his neck served as a reminder of another unsuccessful conflict with our neighbour's crossed-eyed cat, Clarence.

As the shabby animal sat observing us through his solitary eye, Sandy insisted, 'He'll have to go.'

'No!' I protested. 'I've had him nearly all of my life.'

'Well,' she said placing her hands on her hips and smiling playfully, 'it's make your mind up time. It's either me or him.'

I knew that by agreeing to her ultimatum I was condemning myself to being continually bossed about and browbeaten for the rest of our relationship. Then I smelt her perfume and reluctantly leaned down to pick up the soft toy.

'Come on, old son,' I said with a heavy heart. 'Daddy's got a new friend. She looks and smells nicer than you and I know she'll keep me warm at night.' Cradling him lovingly, I walked across the room, kissed him, and placed him in his new home on top of the wardrobe.

We started unpacking again and placed her clothes into the space I had cleared earlier. Every man knows that when a woman agrees to move in, he has to compromise. The more space you allow, the more they want. The takeover was nearly complete when she finished matching and aligning her shoes in the bottom of the cupboard. She slammed the door before saying with satisfaction, 'That's sorted. That leaves just the one case.'

I was lolling at the foot of the bed, watching in wonderment as she completed this feat of engineering as only a woman could. Sandy was sitting at a right angle to me and a small open suitcase was between us. She opened the top drawer of her bedside cabinet and started to put in handfuls of her lingerie. The sight of her shocking-pink, midnight-black and electric-blue bras and pants served only to fire up my engine. Then she pulled out a flaming-red frilly garment and dangled it teasingly in front of me.

My jaw dropped and I asked, 'What's that?'

She leaned closer and whispered, 'It's a suspender belt. I might show you later, but only if you are a good boy.' She giggled impishly then, without warning, sprang to her feet and moved to the end of the bed. Towering over me, she nudged my yielding knees apart with hers, placed her hands lightly on my shoulders and pressed me down.

'No, I can't. It's not right. I feel awkward,' I whimpered. 'Cecil is watching.'

An expression of disbelief spread across her face. She bounced back up and strode purposefully to the wardrobe. Reaching up, she grabbed the soft toy and roughly turned his face to the wall then returned to the bed and resumed her position.

I put my arms around her and held her, smelling the intoxicating aroma of her hair and feeling her hot, sweet breath on my neck. We lay suspended in time, not daring to move or hardly breathe. I truly believed at that moment that heaven really is a place on earth.

Gradually I became aware of her chest pounding against mine, her hips thrusting and legs squeezing. We remained tightly entwined and fully clothed while she writhed up and down slowly on top of me.

'God, oh my God, oh my good God,' I moaned orgasmically – but it was too late.

CHAPTER 15

Gone to the Dogs

Still half asleep on the second Saturday morning in March, I rolled onto my side and reached out my right hand. I felt only emptiness; Sandy's recent departure from the bed was evidenced by the still-warm sheet.

As the mist began to clear in my mind, it was replaced by the two familiar yet unwelcome demons of insecurity and paranoia. Where had she gone? Why had she gone? When did she leave? What was the reason? Who was she meeting? I needed to know in order to appease my anxiety and soothe my overactive imagination. Recently there had been occasional evenings when I couldn't contact her that she would not explain.

I threw aside the duvet and got up, snatched my well-worn dressing gown, which lay crumpled on the floor and dizzily headed for the door. It was at that point, I remembered from the previous evening, Sandy had told me she was due in work at nine o'clock. She would have had to rise at eight to get ready before walking the short distance to the shop.

She had been in a particularly foul mood all the previous day, informing me that she was tired, emotional, had a throbbing headache and a sore and swollen stomach. When at last we were in bed, I tried to alleviate her discomfort by offering to rub her back and give her a cuddle. She had made it very clear that I was neither to touch her nor make any amorous advances.

When I went into the bathroom, I noticed the leg of a pair of tights hanging limply over the rim of a wicker washing basket. As my reasoning gradually returned, the theory that she had abandoned me didn't hold water; she would be unlikely to leave her dirty laundry behind. My spirits lifted further when, ignoring the pink toothbrush which rested in the yellow plastic beaker, I selected my blue one. I was on the point of starting to brush my teeth when I spotted the explanation for her short temper. In the centre of the shelf above the sink rested an opened box of bullet-shaped tampons alongside a packet of sanitary towels, surrounded by various lotions, potions and pills. Never, I suspect, has a man drawn so much relief from realising the significance of such feminine items. My joy was complete when, raising my gaze to the mirror on the wall, I saw written in lipstick in capital letters the words, 'I LOVE YOU.' Little things mean so much.

Sometime later, I continued the weekly ritual of placing my football bet at the local bookies. This habit had been unbroken for nearly four years; this season, in particular, had proved fruitless and I was convinced that if I threw a fiver up into the air, it would land as a court summons. I was certainly overdue a bonanza.

Coming under starter's orders, I trotted out into the mild day. The main road was already busy with traffic. The pavements were bustling with shoppers, elbowing and shouldering me off the kerb. Pushing open the heavy glass door of the betting shop, I entered and observed that it was packed with men diligently studying the form of the dogs and horses in the hope of swelling their coffers. The pungent aroma of the great unwashed was stomach-wrenching.

I strode resolutely to the counter and, ignoring the first cashier, slid the completed betting slip to Sandy. 'I read your message written on the mirror,' I whispered.

She smiled warmly and said, 'I meant it. I'm really sorry about last night as well.'

'Don't worry about it,' I replied and waved a dismissive hand.

She leaned forward with her face almost touching the protective glass and lowered her voice. 'I'll see you tonight.'

'What time?' I mouthed softly.

'Around six,' she replied.

'OK, I'll see you later.' I flipped my scanned receipt back towards her. 'You look after that. I've had no success in ages. Let's see if you can do better.' Then I set off back home for a relaxing afternoon in front of the television.

Around teatime, I had just gone into the kitchen to make a hot drink when the sudden ringing of my mobile forced me to rush across the lounge. After swiping the screen and recognising Sandy's number, I said, 'Hi babe.'

'Guess what? You won't believe it! Your bet has won,' she said excitedly.

'What!'

'Your bet has won,' she repeated.

'No way!'

'Yes!' she confirmed. 'Marjorie has just settled it. You've got £85.'

'No way,' I repeated in disbelief.

'Didn't you watch the final football scores?'

'No, I was watching a film and just about to get a coffee.'

'Yes, they all won.'

'That's fantastic! I'm buzzing. I knew letting you hold the ticket would change my fortunes. Bring the winnings with you when you come home and we'll treat ourselves to a takeaway.'

'That will make a nice change,' she said.

Then I thought of another plan. 'Actually, why don't we celebrate and have a night out at the dogs?'

'For real? What a wicked idea. I've never been before. It will be fab.'

Still in a high state of excitement after returning home, Sandy hung her bag and coat in the cupboard and bounded across the room before diving on top of me as I lay sprawled on the sofa. With the fears and uncertainties of the morning firmly behind me, I returned her affectionate kisses. Then, slightly altering her position, she snatched the wad from her back pocket before teasingly tickling the tip of my nose with the cash. 'I knew I'd be lucky for you,' she said sniffing and kissing the notes. 'I love money, really love money. By hook or by crook I'll be rich one day, you mark my words.'

Suddenly, Sandy sprang to her feet and, still flaunting my winnings, said, 'This is mine; I'm going to keep it,' while beckoning me to follow. I leapt up from the settee to chase her as she backed into the bedroom. We rolled around playfully like a couple of Cumberland wrestlers until she surrendered and handed over the wedge. But that was only half the prize I wanted. I stayed on top of her, panting, before starting to kiss her.

A few moments later, she whispered, 'I can't. You know I can't.'

'I know,' I empathised. 'But there are other things we can do together.'

Two hours later, and with a satisfied smile on my face, we arrived at the Belle Vue Greyhound Stadium. We'd missed the first three races on the card. We decided to sit indoors rather than stay outside with the few hardy souls who were dotted around the perimeter of the track in the cold night air.

The grandstand was reasonably full but we managed to find a table at the window on the first floor. This gave us a panoramic view of the arena. The multicoloured lights on the tote betting board and the indecipherable gesturing of the tic-tacs and arm-waving of the bookmakers presented a very theatrical picture.

We sat close together, studying the race card. The aims of nights such as these are, of course, to have some fun but mainly to back a winner or two. Sadly, I had never managed to master the art of picking winners. Greyhounds and racehorses posed a seemingly impossible mystery; even the unfathomable form guide offered little assistance because the various comments offered up by the resident tipster served only to further cloud the issue. The dog's breeding, Irish form, trial times, preferred going, optimum race weight, recent form figures and likely odds would have baffled an emeritus professor. We needed the help of someone who was experienced in unravelling such conundrums by clear thinking and solid logic; what we did not need was an enthusiast or an expert. We wanted a specialist.

'All right yous two? What are yous doing here?' slurred a man's voice. Glancing up from the race card I saw, to my dismay, that it was Biffo from the local betting shop. Clutching a half-empty bottle of beer, he was wearing a grubby white T-shirt bearing a picture of a greyhound, with a slogan in black lettering reading 'I LOVE DOGGING'. To his right was a woman of around the same age with slightly more grey hair and an equally chubby face, who was lovingly clinging onto a pint of cheap cider. She looked as though she had been poured into her dress, with plenty spilling out.

'Hello,' I replied. 'How are you?'

'Yeah, sweet, man. Sweet.' Biffo extended a grimy paw before gesturing towards his girlfriend and introducing her as Linda. It seemed that they had met at a Scottish country dancing class and were now having a fling. She offered her hand to Sandy, who appeared startled and somewhat reluctant to accept.

In an effort to be friendly, I suggested they join us for a drink. When they each pulled out a chair, I felt Sandy deliver a sharp kick to my left shin. She gave me a withering look that inferred there would be no special treats for me later that night.

Biffo drunkenly but passionately burbled about the forthcoming races. He was a devotee of greyhound racing; of course, this did not guarantee him a winning selection but he stood more of a chance than us. Linda sat opposite him, as though constrained by a straitjacket, and appeared as cheerful as a mass murderer waiting on death row.

After ten minutes or so of effing and blinding, Biffo rose unsteadily and prepared to leave. 'Don't forget,' he said confidently, while leaning into me and belching a putrid mixture of alcohol, tobacco and fried onions disgustingly into my face. 'Trap one in the tenth race. It's a certainty. It can't lose, I guarantee. The more you put on - boom - the more you get back.' Then they stumbled away, arm in arm for mutual support, in an attempt to rediscover the bar and recommence their beerathon.

Sandy wrinkled her brow and spoke first. 'That's blown it. That tosser will tell everyone he's seen us together. He's full of gossip and innuendo.' She turned her palms to the sky in exasperation.

Attempting to pacify her, I said, 'Well, people were bound to find out in the end.'

'I tried so hard to keep this a secret from everyone. I don't like anyone in the shop knowing my business,' she said reproachfully.

'People will find out, won't they?'

'I suppose so,' she conceded stroppily. She looked daggers as she finished her drink and banged her glass down in frustration.

Undeterred by our losing streak, we stayed until the tenth race to see whether Biffy Nostradamus could strike gold. We had already frittered away five pounds each on the previous four contests so, bearing in mind my earlier good fortune, 'Mike's Moneymaker' must be a sure thing.

We decided to watch the final race from outside. The night air was noticeably cooler than earlier as we watched the greyhounds walk in front of the watching crowd. The close-up inspection gave the punters an opportunity to view these canine athletes, before gambling their hard-earned cash.

The trap one runner was very frisky as he paraded past us in his red racing jacket. He was barking like a market trader, bouncing like a rubber ball and propelling his tail furiously like a windmill in a gale-force wind; I am sure he winked at me in an effort to encourage my financial support. Already in arrears, I boldly decided to place a twenty-pound bet on our selection at odds of 4/1.

The unreliability of greyhound racing was demonstrated when the mechanical hare approached the starting traps before triggering the system that released the dogs. All six raced eagerly to the first turn. Unfortunately there was a bit of a fracas, from which two dogs managed to escape and were left clear of the pack. The bitch wearing the blue jacket held a slender advantage approaching the final corner but our dog in red was gaining ground on the inside. A tremendous buckle took place around the final bend and all the way up the home straight before 'Mike's Moneymaker' forced his head in front shortly before the line and stayed on strongly to win, albeit a shade cosily.

Throughout the contest I was oblivious to the shouting and cheering of the other spectators. As it became apparent that trap one was going to prevail, I became aware of Sandy jumping up and down and squealing with delight. Triumphantly, I turned to her and asked, 'What do you think of that, babe?'

'It was brilliant,' she said, eyes flashing wildly and performing a mini fist pump. Then, giddy with success, she asked, 'How much have we won?'

'A hundred pounds,' I confirmed.

'Oh great, that's fifty pounds each,' she said. Fifty pounds each, I thought. She's not had her purse out all evening, not bought a drink nor paid for any of the previous bets, and that last twenty-pound bet was my money.

Given the scenario of every man labouring under the misapprehension that he has had a result, I remembered the old adage muttered by every woman in this position: 'What's yours is mine and what's mine's my own.'

CHAPTER 16

Questions Galore

Driving away from the chaotic, ever-competitive but spiritually crushing sales office, as twilight trickled across the suburban skies and the gloom gathered on that windy Wednesday teatime, I started to mull over the relatively serene progress of our fledgling relationship. As I waited at the traffic lights, I also ruminated on the current state of the alliance since Sandy had moved in earlier in the month.

From the tricky dialogue and embarrassing shyness, which are features of most embryonic friendships, we now felt totally at ease with one another. In fact, I joked to myself, things were going so well that we were in grave danger of escalating into a boring, staid and stereotypical married couple. No doubt in time I would develop a paunch, grow a beard and refer to my peers as 'Young Man' before graduating to complaining about the weather, moaning at the price of beer and constantly visiting the bathroom during the small hours. Meanwhile, Sandy would become my wife, put on two stone and stop dressing in short skirts, before descending into old age and starting to make jam.

Thankfully the lights changed to amber and then green, which prevented me from descending any further into despair at the gruesome prospect. I accelerated away and buried the disturbing and unappealing images firmly in the recesses of my mind.

Soon after, while stuck behind a slow-moving wide load with brakes that squealed like a piece of chalk on a blackboard, I observed the proliferation of convenience stores, fast-food takeaways and already pulsating bars which stretched far into the distance, as their welcoming thresholds spilt illumination onto the litter strewn and bustling pavements. The drawn-faced, hunch-shouldered and bent-backed members of the public, belted, buckled and wrapped against a harsh easterly, trudged solemnly back to the warmth and comfort of their homes, where dinners were prepared, work stories shared, before bedtime was declared.

The strong wind indiscriminately swirled and twirled the used chocolate wrappers, empty crisp packets and discarded burger boxes under the trundling and unforgiving wheels of cars, vans and lorries. Fleetingly, I imagined how different this modern scene of daily drudgery might have looked sixty years ago. The well-maintained road, currently choked and plagued by diesel-belching vehicles packed tightly together, would have been preceded by a cobbled street, little – if any – pollution and negligible congestion. The multitude of colourfully lit late-opening retail outlets would have replaced drab-looking businesses which routinely closed at five o'clock. The thronged walkways would have been sparsely populated by residents who were either late for their tea or early for evensong, I surmised, before turning into Primrose Avenue, tired, hungry and yearning for the gentle touch which had been promised in a salacious text, received at lunchtime.

My sweetheart was already preparing for the evening when I arrived home. I put the remnants of a mass-produced shepherd's pie and mixed veg in the microwave and bolted it down before shaving, showering and dressing. The grey T-shirt which I chose to wear proudly reminded the football and wider world of the goal-scoring exploits of Ole Gunnar Solskjaer during the 1999 Champions League Cup Final, held in Barcelona. My fading blue jeans hung loosely due to my slight weight loss, but the big buckled belt provided me with the peace of mind that they would not fall to the floor. My attire was completed by a recently whitened pair of trainers. Sandy, however, was dressed in a fitted cream blouse, black leather trousers and new canvas shoes. We put on our fleeces before sallying forth arm in arm to walk the short distance to the pub.

That year St Patrick's Day coincided with the weekly pub quiz at the Golden Lion. The relatively simple examination of general knowledge and current affairs tended to attract mainly groups of students who thought they knew better, teams of teachers who should have known better and a confusion of pensioners who did not know better. The winner's cash prize of £50 was keenly contested but, unfortunately, my two previous efforts to be crowned champion had ended in failure. I placed the blame for only achieving mid-table mediocrity squarely on the shoulders of my teammates. However, I was determined that this time the result would be different. I had replaced the underachievers with Sandy, Jessica and her latest boyfriend, Gordon.

A crescent-shaped moon was shining brightly in the velvety night sky. The raw March winds had returned from earlier in the week but at least it was dry. We arrived at the pub, where the other half of our team was sheltering against the cold near the entrance. Jessica hugged Sandy like a long-lost sister before turning her attention to me. We embraced mechanically, like two figures that come out of a clock on the hour.

Gordon was a typically dressed student. Zipped inside a shabby parka, he was pale and wiry with unkempt hair enhanced by gel; it seemed he had forgotten or neglected to shave. 'Hi, I am Gordon,' he sneered nasally, while extending his hand that was more slippery than a Google accountant's.

'Hello, I'm Mike,' I replied.

When we were inside, I noticed the walls were adorned by dozens of small Irish flags and shamrocks made from coloured paper. A clutch of plastic leprechauns stood guard along the length of the bar, while a matching carpet and curtains added to the sea of green. A U2 song reverberated from the speakers as a Bono lookalike prepared for his cabaret spot later in the evening.

The atmosphere resembled that of a venue in Dublin's Temple Bar rather than central Manchester. The Tavern was full of phonies claiming to be of Irish descent because they had once read James Joyce, occasionally drunk a pint of Guinness or adhered to the Catholic faith. It seemed strange that a so obviously English pub went to a lot of time and trouble in celebrating the patron saint of Ireland, when on the twenty-third of April there would be no reference to our equivalent.

We established ourselves at a spindly table. Sandy and Jessica sat cradling double gin and tonics, completely engrossed in chatting about everything which had happened since Sandy's departure from their shared flat. Gordon and I stared disinterestedly at each other and nursed pints of the 'Black Stuff' while desperately trying to think of something to say.

I spoke first. 'So what are you studying, then?'

'Sociology,' he replied.

Of course you are. What else would it be, I thought.

A weighty pause passed before, in an effort to resurrect the conversation, Gordon asked, 'So what's your line of business?'

'I work for a double glazing company,' I responded.

'Are you a salesman, then?' he asked accusingly.

'Yes,' I replied, while thinking that I was not a very successful one at the moment. Commission is hard to earn. After another short interlude, I enquired, 'Whereabouts are you from originally?'

'I come from Milton Keynes,' he replied proudly, puffing out his pigeon chest.

'Milton Keynes,' I repeated. 'Named in honour of the poet andthe economist?'

'Yeah, yeah. That Pam Ayres or Robert Peston or something,' he said, failing to understand the joke. This verbal exchange convinced me that Gordon really was a moron.

The quiz started on time and consisted of the usual eclectic mixture of forty questions. Some were difficult like, *Which planet has a moon called Larissa?* Some were easy, such as: *What is the third colour of the rainbow?* Some were downright impossible. Initially hamstrung by our age, failure to comprehend Latin and unfamiliarity with the works of Shakespeare, we struggled in the first part of the competition but we came into our own when it was time for the geography and sport sections. The relatively easy answer to the question: *Which football team won the 1999 European Champions League Cup Final?* appeared to stump the sociologist, even though the answer was proudly displayed on the front of my T-shirt. After blinking owlishly and frowning intensely, he looked up for inspiration, down in desperation and sideways for information until his girlfriend pointed at my top and realisation dawned.

'Derrr,' he said, putting his head in his hands before pounding his thigh in frustration. 'I should have known that one. I like soccer.'

We achieved an honourable third place, which was an improvement on past performances. It had been a pleasant enough few hours – if you disregarded the company.

Gordon appeared more enthusiastic than the rest of us, as evidenced by his eager lunge forward. He offered his clammy paw and gushed, 'That was awesome, fantastic! We must do it again.' Not likely, I thought. He gave Sandy a quick peck on the cheek before Jessica stepped forward and gave me the same. She then flung her arms around Sandy's neck and the two beautiful and gin-insulated girls held on tightly, as though they were unlikely ever to meet again. When they finally parted, our companions for the evening linked arms and staggered away towards the nearby halls of residence.

When we were back home, we could hear an

enthusiastic prayer group who met in the apartment across the landing and seemed to participate in a sort of ritual chanting. I could not make out the words, though Sandy seemed to think that they revolved around the demise of the West. Ignoring the irritation, I went into the kitchen, flicked on the kettle and prepared to make a nightcap. 'What do you want to drink, babe?' I shouted.

'I'll have a hot chocolate, hon,' she replied.

It was at that point that I decided it was the right time to pop the question about the thorny subject that had been exercising my brain for the past couple of weeks. After all, we were two souls in the same boat, so perhaps we should start pulling together.

Carefully carrying the mugs into the lounge, I set them down on a low wooden coffee table, before flopping down wearily and placing my arm around Sandy's shoulders. She snuggled up affectionately. Edgily, I took hold of her hand before saying with a trembling voice, 'I want to ask you something.'

She lifted her head and listened attentively. 'What do you want to ask me, hon?'

'Well,' I began, before drawing a deep breath and dropping to the carpet on one knee. 'Recently I've been doing a lot of thinking. Now that we live together, we seem to have settled in together. We like each other, we have a lot in common, we want to be together—'

'Yes, yes,' she interrupted impatiently, in an effort to hurry me along.

'OK,' I continued. 'Are you prepared to make a financial contribution towards the mortgage?'

The air went out of the balloon. She sighed, closed her eyes and, as the words sank in, I saw her dejection in her sagging shoulders. She considered briefly before saying, 'Yes, of course. I've been thinking about it. It's only fair that I should help out if we're living together. It's not a problem.' After another pause she added, 'Now that I live here, I don't have to pay for student digs and with the weekend wages from the bookies, it's not an issue. Why don't we set up a joint bank account?' she suggested practically. 'Everything can be paid in and out of it. It will make things a lot easier.'

'OK, that sounds a good idea. I'll contact the bank tomorrow and sort it out.'

Sliding to the floor and kissing me tenderly, she said, 'I thought you were going to ask something totally different.'

CHAPTER 17

Bank on Me

On the afternoon before Good Friday, I had organised some time off from work in order to keep an appointment at the bank. Approaching the small local branch, it was possible to see in the distance that the entrance was partially obscured by a spaghetti of scaffolding, which stood tall and erect as it climbed redundantly into the sunlit and azure sky. After navigating through the metal mishmash and entering the bare-walled, high-ceilinged and strobe-lit open-plan room, which afforded no privacy to the line of queuing clients, I observed on the right-hand side an elderly woman fighting a frustrating but, ultimately, unsuccessful battle with the cashpoint, despite the attentions of an overweight, ponytailed, constantly coughing male assistant.

A scary-looking female with smooth dark hair, which was touched by age that she made no attempt to disguise, wearing a severe black suit and spectacles, sat like a schoolmistress behind a highly polished desk. As Sandy and I approached, she inclined her head and, assuming a look of bored indifference, asked in a monotone, 'Can I help you?'

'Yes,' I replied. 'We have a two o'clock meeting.'

She tapped speedily on the computer keyboard and demanded, 'Name?'

'Carpenter, Michael Carpenter.'

She searched through the list of appointments until she found the right file and ticked the appropriate box, then instructed us to sit on the flimsy chairs opposite her work station.

'My name is Margaret,' she said. 'I will help you complete your application to add a name to your account, before processing the forms.'

After a short time rummaging in her drawer for the relevant paperwork, she asked, 'Why do you wish to include another person on your record?'

'Now that we've moved in together, we've decided to share the mortgage, split the household expenses and divide any other bills. It makes more sense if our incomes and expenditure go in and out of the same account.'

'I see,' Margaret said. 'Are you planning to get married soon, formalise your arrangement or put the relationship on a legal footing?'

'We have made no immediate plans. It's not been discussed,' I replied, rather on the back foot.

She turned her attention to Sandy. 'How long have you been cohabiting?'

'About four weeks,' Sandy responded guardedly.

'How long have you known each other?'

'Approximately six months.' Sandy sounded defensive.

'How do you earn a living?'

'I'm a law student but I work weekends and public holidays in a betting shop.'

Our inquisitor rolled her eyes in silent disapproval but carried on filling in the forms.

After three more questions, Margaret glowered at me and summed up the case. 'You wish to add a second signatory to your account, a student that you met recently who occasionally works in the bookies. You are now living together but have no long-term commitment. Have I understood the position correctly?'

'Yes,' I confirmed, thinking that cynicism is the curse of the middle-aged.

'Very well.' She sighed and picked up an A4-sized piece of paper. 'Have you brought any photo ID, Miss Gibson?' she asked.

Sandy delved frantically into her capacious handbag and produced a passport.

'I'll take a copy of this for our records,' Margaret said. 'If you provide two specimen signatures, I should be able to expedite your request.'

Faintly shell-shocked after the bombardment, we stayed silent for a moment. Having completed the formalities, sour-faced Margaret reappeared from the rear office. As she returned the passport, she said, 'I notice you were born in my home town.' This throwaway remark was met by a blush and shrug of the shoulders as Sandy replaced the documents into her bag. The bossy bat added, 'I've ordered an extra chequebook and debit card. They'll be despatched under separate cover within the next five working days.'

We thanked her insincerely and made our escape.

Emerging from the dingy building into the brightness and comparatively fresher air, we burst into laughter. 'What's her problem?' I asked.

'The silly old dragon is probably not getting any,' replied Sandy rather coarsely, but with the manner of someone who was.

'You'd need to be brave to tackle her,' I said, thankful that the ordeal was over.

'I think that stroppy cow is what's called Miss Iron Drawers. Did you notice she didn't wear an engagement or wedding ring? She probably hasn't got a "special friend" and still lives at home,' Sandy speculated cattily.

Sometime later, we were sprawled out at either end of the sofa, watching the early evening news through half-open eyes. Suddenly Sandy announced, 'Jessica is organising a girly weekend abroad at the end of April and I'd like to go.'

Stirring from my apathy, I sat up and asked, 'Where are you going?'

'Benidorm,' she answered, fiddling with her ear.

I had heard friends comparing the eastern Spanish town to Blackpool with sunshine. It had achieved a certain notoriety among British tourists but, for consenting adults, how can you object to their desire for 'fun in the sun' and sand, sea and sangria? But although our new relationship was reasonably stable and seemed to be flourishing, there was still an underlying question of trust lurking in the back of my mind.

'Is there a special reason for the trip?' I enquired, trying to sound casual.

'Not really. It's just to enjoy a girls' get-together. We want to let our hair down and chill out. It's been a long, miserable winter,' Sandy said casually and crossed her legs. For a moment, I fantasised about her wearing a skimpy bikini as she tanned in the sizzling heat while lying lazily on Levante Beach.

'How many people are interested?' I asked.

'I'm not sure. About ten,' she responded.

'When is it?'

'We're hoping to fly out on the final Friday of the month and return early on the Monday. Jessica is in charge of everything. Some of her friends are going and the rest are from uni. I won't get involved if you don't want me to,' she said.

'No, no, if you want to join in with them it's fine by me. I'm cool about it,' I said, trying not to be a killjoy. 'How much will it cost?'

'I'm not sure yet. It depends on how many of us can afford it. She's not worked out the final figure. It won't be expensive.'

'Well, you have a nice time, babes. I don't mind. I'll find something to do.' I placed a reassuring hand on her knee. In turn she put hers on top of mine, thus restricting any further progress along her thigh. I sensed that things were not the same as yesterday and felt a gnawing disquiet.

'I'll have to save up, work extra shifts and economise a bit because I haven't got much spare cash at the moment,' Sandy said.

'Join the club. I got my monthly statement at the start of the week and I'm in the brown again. I'm amazed the lady in the bank didn't mention it when she looked at my details.'

'Are you overdrawn?' she asked anxiously.

'I was at that point, but my salary has gone in so I'm

solvent again. I haven't earned any commission. Times are hard. Surviving on just a basic wage is tricky,' I explained. 'I need some extra money, higher commissions, bigger bonuses. What I really want is something from left field or a better-paid job.'

I mulled over the steps I could take to improve my finances. Sandy must have been reading my mind. 'I have a plan to bridge the current funding gap,' she said.

'What? What is it?'

'Well, Biffo from the shop has got hold of some counterfeit currency and is feeding it into the fixed-odds betting terminal.'

'And…' I prompted.

'If the machine accepts the dodgy money, he plays roulette, blackjack or some other game for very small stakes. Then he presses the withdrawal button and takes the ticket to the cashier for payment.'

'How do you know it's funny money?' I asked with growing fascination.

'There have been security checks recently and we've been told to be vigilant about any unusual betting patterns. The manageress suspects him because he regularly places smallish bets so it's dubious when he cashes a receipt for over £100. I'm certain it's him. He only plays the machines when the shop is full, so it's not as obvious.'

I deliberated for a while on what she had told me. 'Where does he get the Mickey Mouse money from?'

'I'm not sure,' she said, shaking her head. 'I can ask him.'

'You can't just come out with it,' I protested. 'It's tantamount to accusing him.'

'Why don't you question him then?' she suggested.

'You get on with him. He likes you, so he might spill the beans. He's always in during the morning, so come in and quiz him. If not, I'll get his phone number for you. He's a lech; he's bound to give it to me. I know he fancies me.' She paused before continuing, 'Anyhow, there are a few other shops in the area with similar slot machines. You can always use them.'

'Let me think about it,' I said, trying to absorb the idea and analyse its pros and cons. 'It sounds a bit risky.'

'Of course it is! It's deception. It's money laundering.'

Later, Sandy decided to take a bath. I went around the apartment turning off the lights before retiring to the bedroom. Midway through undressing, my eye was drawn to a booklet near her handbag. I leafed through it and noticed that her details were displayed as Sandra Louise Gibson, born 05/05/1989 in Dewsbury. I froze for a moment. I was absolutely positive that she had said her place of birth was Shrewsbury.

I climbed into bed and reached for the thriller I was reading but it was hard to concentrate on the storyline because of the mystery that was closer to home.

When Sandy came into the room, naked and smelling of her favourite sandalwood bath gel, she complained, 'There's not enough hot water to wet the valleys, let alone cover the hills. I just had a quick shower.' She looked young and beautiful and a picture of innocence.

However, instead of keeping my big mouth shut, I shattered the romantic mood by asking, 'Didn't you say you were brought up in Shrewsbury?'

There was an awkward silence during which Sandy looked bemused. Then she fixed me with a steely eye and demanded, 'What do you mean?'

I put down my paperback and replied, 'I was just studying your passport and it states that you were born in Dewsbury.'

The pleasant atmosphere changed dramatically as her eyebrows lowered in a scowl, her lips thinned and the pout vanished from her face. 'Have you been snooping among my things?' she accused tetchily.

'No,' I answered indignantly. 'It was on the dresser. I just glanced through it. I assumed we had no secrets.' My words only inflamed the situation; she looked livid and her ears reddened in rage before she launched into a verbal attack.

'I never said I came from Shrewsbury. I mentioned Dewsbury. Anyway, you have no reason to spy on me. What happened to trust? You shouldn't go through my things; it's bad manners. And you shouldn't keep watching me, it's unnecessary. You should believe me! I don't go through your belongings when you're in the bathroom. You've invaded my personal space and I feel betrayed. You're totally out of order!' she ranted, before grabbing the offending document and ramming it deep into her handbag.

'All right, all right,' I said, trying to defuse the situation. 'It's no big deal. It's probably a misunderstanding. I thought that you said you were brought up in Shrewsbury, but I may have misheard you.'

'Yes, well, now you know. It just shows how much you listen to me. You never pay any attention and you're not interested in what I say.'

She cast me a withering glance before snatching an unflattering flannelette nightie from the wardrobe and yanking it aggressively over her head. She flounced onto the bed, turned to the wall and failed to say goodnight.

Needless to say, I didn't attempt to cross the divide that separated us for the remainder of that unsettled night.

CHAPTER 18

Bunkered

The deafening sound of a slamming front door jolted me from a troubled sleep on that bright and breezy Good Friday morning. Sandy had jumped eagerly at the chance of earning some extra money by working overtime in the shop.

Even after her hasty departure from the apartment, an uncomfortable and frosty atmosphere still prevailed. I stayed in bed for some time, reflecting on the bizarre events of the previous day. I couldn't understand her reaction to the confusion about her place of birth; her melodramatic switch from warm-heartedness to giving me the cold shoulder was baffling. Was she hiding something? Was she telling the truth about her family and upbringing? Was she really what she seemed? All of these questions tormented me as I rolled out of bed, dressed quickly and went into the kitchen.

Placed in the centre of the table was a postcard-sized

piece of paper covered in large, looped handwriting. With my heart beating like a Salvation Army drum, I picked up the note anticipating a Dear John letter. It read: 'Really sorry about last night, hon. I overreacted badly. I shouldn't have spoken to you like that and I apologise. I'll make it up to you later.'

I exhaled loudly with relief. I remembered reading in a book once that 'love is an emotion quite different from ordinary sexual feelings'. Was this love, then, that I was experiencing?

Feeling chipper, and keen for a change of scenery, I strolled through the local park where an early spring breeze was scented with lavender and rosemary, while a skein of geese honked noisily overhead. To the right, a jay clattered in the distant woodland, a willow warbler sang creamily and a white butterfly fluttered flimsily above the bordering hedge. To the left of the pathway, a bunch of bored teenagers kicked furiously at a stamped-out beer can as they dragged like film stars on their cigarettes, no doubt illegally purchased from the neighbouring shop. The sun purred in the mophead canopy of copper beeches, it singularly smirked in the blonde highlights of a young woman yapping at her squatting Shetland terrier and grinned softly on the awakening face of Mother Nature.

Entering the betting shop just before noon, I saw the usual punters optimistically watching the monitors on the whitewashed wall. Sandy was busily serving a line of chancers from her position behind the reinforced glass but it was someone else that I wanted to see.

Biffo was absent-mindedly chewing his thumbnail while leaning lazily against the brown wooden shelf which stretched the length of the wall. Today his baggy, greying T-shirt encouraged the general public to 'Keep on the Grass'.

'Have you got a minute, mate?' I asked.

He stared at me, appearing slightly startled. 'Yeah, man. What is it?'

'Outside,' I said and gestured towards the exit.

Like an obedient sheepdog, he followed as we emerged and walked to the end of the building. We passed the last building in the row, which housed Madam Sin's full-contact massage parlour on the first floor, while below the banging, screwing and nailing continued breathlessly in John's joinery business. We then turned sharply right into a long narrow and dark passageway, which was guarded at the far end by a high, rusting and padlocked gate. The ground was festooned with cigarette ends, greasy takeaway wrappers, discarded pizza boxes, broken glass and crushed plastic cider bottles. An acrid stench, created by men who needed to go, assaulted our nostrils as we loitered among the used rubbers strewn casually on the ground which provided evidence of the activities enjoyed by responsible couples.

'What's happening, man?' Biffo asked, pulling out a pack of smokes and lighting up.

'I've been told you're the man to speak to if I need to get hold of anything around here,' I said, trying to flatter him.

'No, no, not me, man,' he protested. 'I don't do anything heavy; just a bit of weed. I can't help you with anything else.' His face flushed and he stepped away from me.

'I don't mean that,' I exclaimed. 'I'm talking about funny money.'

He raised his eyebrows. 'Funny money?' he repeated.

'What makes you think I can get that?'

'A little bird tweeted in my ear.' I winked and grinned.

'I *thought* you were sleeping with her! I knew something was going on when I saw you both at the dogs.'

'Yeah, well, we're trying to keep it quiet,' I said, raising a finger to my lips.

'I hear you. Your secret is safe with me. I'm no gossip,' Biffo said unconvincingly.

'I believe you,' I lied. 'So, can you get hold of any counterfeit?'

He shifted his feet and dragged anxiously on his cigarette. Then he stared directly at me and asked, 'How much do you want?'

'It depends. How much is it?' I asked,

'A hundred quid's worth will cost you forty quid, but the minimum order is £200, so it will set you back eighty,' he explained.

'OK,' I said slowly. 'When can you get it?'

'Whenever you want.'

'Let me think about it,' I said, unwilling to commit at that moment.

'Sweet man. No sweat. If you're interested, give me a buzz and I'll contact Panda.'

'Who's Panda?' I asked.

'He's the go-to guy, my point of contact. He's a young Chinese kid who does all the printing,' Biffo explained.

'I see,' I responded thoughtfully. 'What's your phone number?' He gave me the details, which I stored in my phone. 'I'll be in touch,' I promised as we retreated from the alleyway before going our separate ways.

After lunch, I went to meet my boss for a prearranged round of golf. During the last six months, he'd been trying unsuccessfully to persuade me to play at his exclusive club. He'd eventually worn me down.

I felt like a duck out of water as I parked my battered old rust bucket among the highly polished, top-of-the-range cars that clogged the car park. My boss was already waiting as I clumsily hoisted my second-hand clubs from the boot. His bald pink head glittered as though it had been waxed when he lolloped over and thrust out a rough right hand. 'Good afternoon, Carpenter. Welcome to my club.'

'Hello to you. Thanks for inviting me,' I responded politely.

As he ushered me to the first tee, he said sadly, 'We can only play half the course today. I've got to be home by six because the in-laws and their kids are coming for hot cross buns. We'll need to get our skates on.'

Even though I had played golf on several occasions, my ability was mediocre, as indicated by my twenty-four handicap. I was certain that I was in for a thorough drubbing. The sales director was a veteran of the sport, having honed his skills over many years of practice. But things don't always work out the way we expect.

We tossed a coin to determine who would tee off and I called incorrectly. Consequently Clive selected a four-iron and addressed the ball. The birds chirped cheerfully in the wooded area to the left of the spongy fairway, oblivious to any potential danger until, suddenly, they scattered for cover as his hooked shot flew into the trees and ricocheted noisily off the timber.

He didn't cry 'fore' or verbally accept the wayward stroke; instead he merely shrugged his shoulders. Time seemed to stand still for a few seconds until I asked, 'Is it my turn now?'

Following his nod of confirmation, I sent a missile right down the middle, which finished some forty yards past my companion. Then I waited for five minutes while Clive searched fruitlessly for his ball in dense woodland. Maybe this game wouldn't be as painful as I had envisaged.

Declaring a lost ball, and under a two-shot penalty, Clive trudged huffily to the tee box, and I finished out in regulation before a concession was begrudgingly granted by the older man.

The second was advertised as a par three and, due to the contours of the lovingly maintained green, my approach rolled thirty feet behind the flag. My opponent, however, bunkered his hybrid and carelessly knifed his second across the undulations and the thick fringe beyond. I took two putts before recording a three on my scorecard, but Clive ecstatically drained his chip to gain a half.

I lost the eighth with a bogey and we were all square going to the daunting ninth, where the man with previous course knowledge boasted that the par five was right up his street as he proceeded to smash a drive into A1 position. I followed suit by flushing my effort to within ten yards of his divot mark, while my long second found the edge of the putting surface. However, his next strike faded to the right and disappeared into a dense, lush hollow. As he looked frantically in the foliage, my heavy-handed third airmailed the dance floor and fizzed into a sand trap.

I climbed into the revetted cavern and looked up with amazement to see that another ball had inexplicably appeared approximately six feet away from the pin. 'Great shot,' I shouted begrudgingly. 'How did you manage that?' I asked, while suspecting some use of the leather wedge.

'Well, you can either play the game or you can't,' Clive said nonchalantly.

I then conjured up a tremendous piece of wizardry, which came to rest less than twelve inches from the target. After scrambling out of the bunker and brushing myself down, I tapped in for a par which left Mr B with a two-yarder for victory.

After nervelessly holing out, Clive embarked on an extraordinary act of celebration. He whirled like a dervish around the green, punching the air with both fists and leaping up and down as though he had single-handedly won the Ryder Cup. When he calmed down, I strolled over and offered my hand, which he shook triumphantly.

'Well played, youngster,' he gloated. 'It's a pity someone has to lose. Let's put these things away and I'll treat you to a beer. I need to have a quick chat, in any case.'

Minutes later we were in the clubhouse. The fully paid-up member bought me a pint while he sipped at a double gin and tonic as we sat at a bay window overlooking the green. After a few minutes' silence, my line manager frowned and leaned towards me. 'There's no easy way of putting this. The accounts department have flagged up a couple of anomalies amongst the petty cash receipts. Apparently some inappropriate and large amounts of money are being claimed and they've asked me to investigate. I told them not to overreact. I'm sure there is a logical explanation but they got on their high horses and started bleating about sackable offences, police involvement, heads rolling, that sort of thing.'

'What's that got to do with me?' I asked, strumming my fingers impatiently on the arm of the chair.

Clive's frown deepened as he resumed. 'We need to get

rid of some dead wood. Trim the wage bill, initiate some synergies. Generally speaking, we need to make swingeing cuts all round.'

A moment of silence elapsed before I asked, 'Do these proposed changes affect me?'

'Well,' he said, 'your sales figures have been heading south for some time. There are other members of the team who I'm considering for release but, as your job is now at risk, I'd start searching elsewhere if I were you. It's nothing personal. You're young, keen and experienced. You won't have any problem finding something new.'

I retreated from the clubhouse and stared gloomily at my ancient car with its sad headlights, treadless tyres and corroding bodywork. It simply glared back at me and challenged me to climb in.

CHAPTER 19

Hatch a Plan

It was a wretched morning with a weeping mist shrouding the streets and houses, I noticed as I drew back the light-blue curtains. Resting my fingers on the recently dusted windowsill, I observed that the now mushy leaves had fallen and formed an impervious plug, which clogged the drains in the road below that were struggling to cope with the sheer deluge of water, and consequently was waiting to dissipate. The flooded grass verges looked like paddy fields as the saturated, overhanging branches of the soaked trees aggrevated the problem by bowing respectfully and dripping their fat raindrops onto the already sodden surface. The leaden skies were mercifully clearing, however, as the first light of dawn penetrated, while the bleak and desolate-looking avenue was devoid of any traffic and humanity as another Saturday started.

'It's only six thirty,' lamented a drowsy female voice. Sandy clicked on her bedside light, stretched luxuriantly and folded her arms behind her head.

'I know,' I said, climbing back into the comfort of the bed. 'But I couldn't sleep properly. All the events of yesterday have been rushing round in my head for hours. I haven't had a wink.'

'I thought as much,' she retorted before placing her head lightly on my chest. 'You kept me awake all night. I'm exhausted.'

'Sorry about that, babes. I know you've got to get up for work soon. I tried to be as quiet as possible but my brain wouldn't switch off. I was going to get up and make a hot drink but I didn't want to disturb you, so I just lay there wrestling with my thoughts.'

'It doesn't really matter. Forget about it. I've been thinking, too. We have a few issues which need airing about employment and money and our future,' she said gravely before kissing my cheek.

'What do you mean? I don't understand.'

Well,' she began seriously, 'with the uncertainty hanging over your current job prospects, as mentioned by your boss yesterday, and the potential dip in income, we will need to tighten our belts. Times will be hard but at least we're in it together. We need money, though, not only to pay the mortgage but also to fund our social life. and possibly, just possibly, a wedding and a family.'

The delicate issues of matrimony and having children had never been discussed during our relationship; in fact, I'd made a conscious effort to steer away from any mention of them because I didn't know how Sandy would react. Despite my father's frequent joking that getting married is like pleading guilty to an indefinite sentence without parole, I believed in marriage. As for offspring, if you are fortunate enough to create a child or two, I believed you were truly blessed. With these thoughts in my mind, I asked, 'Why? Do you want to get hitched and have kids, babe?'

She stared back at me, seeming a little startled. After a pause she regained her composure and called my bluff. 'Is that a proposal, hon?'

'No, not at all. I was just asking. Maybe sometime in the future,' I spluttered, rapidly back-pedalling.

'I was only pulling your leg,' she said and smiled widely.

For the next quarter of an hour, we lay tightly entwined until Sandy asked, 'Are you going to get some of that Mickey Mouse money from Mighty Mouth?'

'Yes, I'm meeting Biffo later today,' I replied, although I was still undecided whether to continue with the foolishness.

'You're not going to get much of a reward, though, are you?'

'Not really,' I said. 'If we get a grand, split it equally and pay his contact £400, that works out at £500 apiece for shelling out only £200 each. If I can get rid of the counterfeit, we've had a right result.'

She hesitated and rolled away from me, propping herself up on her elbow. 'It's only small-time, though, isn't it? We're not going to get rich quick that way. Even if you do it a few times, you're not making much money from your outlay.'

'That's true,' I agreed and sighed wearily. 'But with all the security equipment, it's difficult to shift it. You need to aim precisely at your chosen targets. It may take a bit longer, but at least it's safer.' I had given the idea plenty of consideration over the last twenty-four hours.

'I get that, hon, but it seems like a lot of work for not much reward. What we need is a foolproof plan to get as much money as possible with the minimum of risk. We need to hit the jackpot or pull off the big one,' she concluded. Then Sandy bounced energetically onto to her knees. 'I think I know how to pull it off,' she said.

I looked at her curiously. 'So what is it? What is your strategy, babes?'

'Well,' she began, 'in the betting shop where I work, each completed slip that we accept is processed through a scanner. That transmits a photocopy of the bet to head office before a receipt is generated and given to the customer. The receipt clearly shows a time and date stamp.'

'OK,' I said with interest. 'Then what?'

'So what would happen if there was a power cut, for instance, and the equipment was unable to function?'

'I don't know,' I admitted.

'In that scenario we have a backup system whereby we use a manual stamp before a duplicate is returned to the punter.'

'I see. Then what?'

'If it's a winning bet, the manager will settle it as a valid slip because it displays all the correct details that are needed to satisfy any security check.'

'Right,' I said.

'So, I was thinking. When it's a busy day - on a Saturday afternoon for example - if you give me a blank coupon before the three o'clock kick-off time, I can stamp it manually. After the football matches have finished, you can fill it in with a winning ten-team accumulator and present it to Marjorie for payment,' she said.

I pondered for a moment. 'Why wouldn't you put it

through the scanning machine?'

'That's the key. We need to be either fortunate or to arrange some sort of power outage that would make the machinery useless. Then it doesn't look so obvious when the tickets are processed by hand.'

I immediately detected a flaw in the scam: how could we arrange a power cut? Then, in a moment of inspiration, I suggested, 'What about my brother? He's an electrician. Maybe he could trip a switch or blow a fuse or cut a wire. That would give you sufficient time to mark the empty slip correctly.'

'Do you think he'd want to do it?' she asked, rubbing her chin thoughtfully.

'I'm sure he would if I asked him. But we'd need to give him a bung. He could gain access to the main junction box at the end of the street.'

'Do you want me to act as go-between for you and your brother?' she offered, rather curiously.

'No. He won't do it for you. Anyway, I'm the one with his mobile number. I'll give him a call later and see if he is up for it.'

Never underestimate the power of a woman over a man, I thought, as I analysed the pros and cons of the scheme. Sandy was placing me in an invidious position. She was tempting me not only to deceive her employers but also to distribute counterfeit cash across the local vicinity. However, my options were limited: redundancy loomed large, with the subsequent prospect of no wages coming in. Money can do so much to ease your path through life; without it you are nothing.

Sandy and I had come a long way in a short space of time; we got on well and her affection for me seemed genuine but, without an income, would her enthusiasm diminish? Would she leave me?

On the other hand, if I committed the crimes I would probably need to go on the run from the authorities and no doubt the law would eventually catch up with me. I was not the sort of person to thrive in prison; I had heard of the terrible things that happened in the dolly, done by people who are not very choosy.

This innocent young girl, who had once naively told me that all kittens were fur-covered balls of sunshine, fairies lived at the bottom of the garden and that there was good in everyone, had seemingly metamorphosed into something quite different. Should I stay and follow through with the strategy, or should I escape from the siren before I was trapped in her clutches forever?

When I went into the kitchen, Sandy was dressed and ready for work. She sat ramrod stiff, eagerly tucking into a fry-up. I settled opposite her, frowning deeply. She asked, 'What's the matter with you? Why no smile?'

'Permanent smiles equal white gowns, lots of special tablets and incarceration,' I replied grumpily.

'Oh, it's like that, is it? You look fed up.'

'I'm all right. I was just thinking about our conversation.' I picked up my cutlery.

'We don't have to do it if you don't want to or if you're not interested. I just thought it would be an easy way of getting a decent amount of quick money. It's up to you; there's no pressure. Anyway,' she said, expertly changing the topic, 'don't forget that I'm going out tonight with the girls and I'll be back late, so you will have to get your own tea.'

'Oh, yes, I forgot,' I confessed. 'If you're going to be

out till late, United are on TV this evening so I'll go and watch it in the pub. I'll get something to eat after that.'

'Fine. I'll see you when I see you.' She leaned forward and pecked me on the forehead. 'Let me know how you get on with Biffo, won't you? And give that other project some consideration,' she ordered, before pulling on her coat, slinging her bag over her shoulder and slamming the front door noisily in her wake.

CHAPTER 20

The Chinese Laundry

The Easter Saturday lunchtime weather had transformed from the earlier sodden scene into a bright and pleasant afternoon as I kept my appointment outside the local betting shop. Predictably, Biffo arrived late. He was unwashed, unshaven and clad in a creased and sweat-stained cream T-shirt tucked untidily into his wrecked jeans. 'I see you've made a big effort, then,' I remarked sarcastically as I eyed him.

'Yeah, I'm knackered, man.' He stretched and yawned expansively to reveal his unbrushed, nicotine-stained teeth. 'I tied one on last night and I've got a thicky to prove it.'

'Don't blame me. It's your own fault. You should know better at your age. We just had a quiet evening in with a bottle of wine.'

'What, with that bird from the bookies?'

'Yes, with Sandy. You know that we are living together,'

I said defensively.

'You told me yesterday but I've kept it under my hat, like you asked.'

'That's fine,' I replied. 'It's what she prefers. She doesn't want anyone to find out.'

'No problem, man. Your secret's safe with me.'

As we strode in the weak spring sunshine, my companion occasionally bumped shoulders with me as he zigzagged across the pavement. We progressed along the formerly downbeat, downgrade and downmarket gritty streets of the inner city, where the most vulnerable, the poorest and those struggling to survive used to live. The once economically and socially deprived area, lacking in ambition, hope and purpose, abandoned by local, regional and national government, was being slowly regenerated into something totally different through grants gratefully received from the European Union. The previously run-down housing estates, neglected schools and disregarded hospitals were undergoing a complete facelift, while the infrastructure of the failed transport network was being completely overhauled. This formerly godforsaken pit of a place was gradually becoming a most desirable location.

When we reached the steps to our destination, Biffo asked, 'Have you brought the dough?'

'Yes. I got £200 out of the ATM, thinking that if we grab a grand and split it equally, it will cost us £400.'

'Yeah, yeah, man. I've got a two-er as well, so give me your dosh and leave the talking to me,' he ordered. 'This guy can be a bit prickly sometimes but at least he knows me. I'll try to nip him for a few quid by offering £350. I'm sure he'll throw his toys out of the pram, but I can handle him. He's a pussycat really, so keep it zipped. It will turn into a "who blinks first" contest, but I've dealt with him before so I know he'll crack eventually.'

Unconvinced by his brash confidence and full of trepidation, I followed him down the narrow, steep flight of steps and pushed open a heavily scuffed door, which led into a strange-smelling printers. A man in his late twenties, small in stature and with oriental features – and, as I discovered after offering my hand, a missing arm – looked up from where he was busily working. I was surprised when he asked in an unexpected Mancunian accent, 'All right, lads. What can I do for yous?'

My companion edged forward cautiously and announced, 'It's me, Panda. It's Biffo.'

The Chinese chap looked at me and demanded suspiciously, 'And who's this character?'

Before I could answer, Biffo intervened. 'He's all right. He's with me and he's cool. We've just come for a little transaction, if you know what I mean.'

Panda nodded approvingly and glanced towards the back office as he bossily instructed his assistant to, 'Mind the shop for a bit while I deal with these two.'

Once inside the cramped, uncarpeted box of a room, the owner locked the door before asking, 'What do you want to buy? Is it weed or money?'

'Just cash, man, but we only want a thousand,' said Biffo.

'Fair enough. That'll cost £400, then.' Panda fumbled in his pocket for a set of keys.

'Four?' objected Biffo. 'Last time I came you said that you'd give me a discount. I've only got three and a half on me.'

'No, I never,' protested the younger man. 'You know

how much it is. It's £200 worth for eighty sterling, so if you need £1,000 I want four ton.' He was becoming annoyed but standing his ground. The uncomfortable silence only lasted a few seconds but it seemed as though several minutes had passed.

'We haven't brought enough, then. I think you're out of order, not honouring your promise from last time. You know me; I'm a regular customer. I introduce others to you. You never get any trouble from me and I shift some blow for you as well. You're bang out of order.' Biffo's neck reddened and his cheeks flushed.

'All right, all right, give me what you've got. But I feel like you've striped me. You've mugged me in my own back yard. Next time, bring the right amount of bread or we won't do business,' Panda stated.

He went behind the bureau, lifted a corner of the lino and opened a safe which was built into the ground. When he had finished rummaging in the dark hole, he straightened and slapped a bundle of unused twenties onto the cluttered desk. 'It's all there. It's all pukka, freshly printed and untraceable.'

Biffo peeled off the required amount of genuine currency from a wad which was thick enough to choke a donkey and fanned out the notes.

Panda said, 'I thought you'd only got £350.'

Biffo, having anticipated the question, explained, 'The rest is for my rent, man. I've got to give it to my mother. She'll kick me out if I don't tip up this week.'

Panda shrugged resignedly, picked up the loot and, without counting it, stuffed it securely into his trousers.

As we escaped unscathed, I felt an awesome wave of relief wash over me. We strolled unhurriedly back home, feeling as delighted as a dog with a dinosaur bone. 'What was that peculiar sickly smell in there?' I asked naively.

'It's opium, man. What did you think it was?' asked Biffo, matter-of-fact.

'He's into that as well, is he?'

'He does anything you want. Whatever you like, he can get it. He's the man.'

'Has he ever been nicked?' I asked.

'Yeah, loads of times, but they can't pin anything on him. He's untouchable. Everyone knows him, where he is and how to get hold of him. I think the cops aren't bothered, they just turn a blind eye. Somewhere along the line they are probably involved with his money laundering, drug trafficking and whatever else he does. After all, they know where the takers and snatchers go.'

'Shall we try a hair of the dog?' I suggested. 'We can go in the Shakespeare, just along here on the left.' I pointed to a black-and-white half-timbered pub.

'Great, why not?' With renewed energy, Biffo tossed his dog end carelessly into the gutter. 'That's the pub they named the playwright after, innit, man?' I could not believe it; his ignorance knew no bounds. With a head like a locked box, he really was as thick as a docker's sandwich.

A bespectacled battleaxe sat on a bar stool, boring the barman about her book club. We found a secluded corner where we drank pints of Czech lager from tall flower vases and ate packets of sea salt and balsamic vinegar crisps. My partner in crime surreptitiously passed my share of the readies under the table into my waiting hand. 'Nice one,' I said, shoving the bundle safely into my pocket.

'Just be careful where you offload it,' Biffo warned. 'A lot of these places have security cameras and detection equipment. When you choose your target, aim accurately and make sure you don't miss.'

'Got you,' I nodded. 'Where would you recommend are the best places to start?'

'Obviously not in here,' he chuckled while glancing around shiftily. 'I'd stick to market stalls, taxis or anywhere where loads of wonga is changing hands quickly and there's less time for any thorough checking to take place. Don't forget the machines in the bookies. They're a dead cert.'

'The girls in the shop are on to you so I'd give it a swerve for a while,' I said, offering a warning.

'I thought they were. Did your little friend tell you?' Biffo appeared slightly put out.

'Yes, she mentioned it a few days ago, but head office is also sniffing around so I'd be very careful.'

'Thanks for the tip-off, man.' Biffo downed the last of his drink and rose steadily before belching, patting his substantial belly and leaving the pub.

A little later that day, I washed and changed before travelling by cab to the heart of the city. Two hours previously, I had contacted a couple of work colleagues and arranged to meet them in the big pub near the canal to watch the teatime football match. The game was largely uneventful and, as a result, ended in a goalless draw.

As I was about to leave, I felt a strong hand from behind me wrap playfully around my throat. I looked up and, to my surprise, saw sausage-fingered Freddy 'with a y' grinning down at me. He said gruffly, 'Now then, young man, what you doing in here?'

I rose hastily from the stool to face him. 'The same as you, I imagine: watching United struggle and enjoying a beer. I haven't seen you for a while. What have you been up to?'

'I've been working in Spain on a building project. Short-term contract, excellent pay, if you get my drift,' he explained, while swaying like a gibbet and fiddling with his flies. 'What did you think of the match?'

'It was rubbish. The whole team are playing poorly at the moment.'

'I know,' he agreed. 'I can't see them winning the league, the cup or even qualifying for Europe this season. They've never been the same since the old manager retired.' He took a greedy sup from his pint pot. 'Anyway,' he continued and sprayed spittle into my face, 'I've not seen you in here before.'

'I'm just having a few scoops with some workmates.'

'I see. I thought you'd be having a pint with your kid,' Freddy remarked curiously.

'No, he lives in Sheffield. He doesn't come over here; he's a home bird.'

Freddy scratched his balding pate thoughtfully. 'I've just seen him in the Grapes along there,' he informed me, extending his right arm and pointing.

'In the Grapes? I don't think so,' I echoed.

Freddy looked bewildered. 'That was your bro who came in the Brickies with you a few months ago, wasn't it? The one with the Sheffield Wednesday sweatshirt and an owl on the front? A big guy, thickset, with a mop of black hair?'

'Yes, it sounds like him,' I admitted, 'but he wouldn't come over without telling me. He just stays local.'

'I'm sure it was him. I waved and he raised his thumb. He was larking about with a fit piece.'

'No, I don't believe it. It can't be him,' I said, mystified.

'Maybe I was mistaken,' Freddy concluded before sauntering off for a refill.

I drained my glass, said goodbye to my friends and rushed towards The Grapes. If the devil was a drinker, he would have been in this cavernous hellhole with the drunken, incoherent scores of bladdered boozers. My sibling was nowhere to be seen.

Retreating to the cooler air outside, I called Kieran's mobile but it was switched off. I sent a text message, which received no reply. With mounting anxiety, I telephoned my parents' house, only to be greeted by an answering machine. Why would my brother be here on a Saturday night? Why hadn't he told me that he was coming across? Which girl was he meeting? And why was he not responding to calls or texts?

For the next hour I wandered aimlessly, seeking answers in the bars and bistros and brasseries for something I wasn't sure about. Finally I returned home in a bone-shaking taxi which stank of cheap perfume, chilli sauce and discarded chips. When I asked, the driver pulled over and stopped near my home. I jumped out and paid him with a forged twenty-pound note and stood with hand outstretched, waiting jumpily for the change.

At just gone ten o'clock, and still in a state of uncertainty, I mounted the steps and let myself into the cold, dark and empty apartment.

CHAPTER 21

Prepare to Succeed

Early on Easter Sunday morning, I woke with an unpleasant sense of doom and foreboding as I recalled the unresolved questions of the previous day. The darkness dwelt intolerably, like an unwanted guest lurking on the threshold, as I tossed and turned in my bed, a galaxy of thoughts drifting dreamily through my brain. Was the reported sighting of my brother in a city centre pub correct and, if so, who was his mysterious and attractive female companion? Why had he neglected to inform me that he was visiting the area? Why had he failed to answer his phone, reply to texts and not respond to voicemails?

For my own sanity, I needed to immediately lift the shroud of mystery which hung like a London fog over the incomprehensible questions, unbelievable circumstances and unexplained situation; after all, I considered profoundly, a deeper understanding leads to a greater piece of mind.

I slid a tentative hand across the bottom sheet until, with relief, my outstretched fingertips found the warmth and silkiness of Sandy's sleeping body. However, this woke her up and she demanded, 'What are you doing? What do you want? What time is it?'

Glancing blearily at the alarm clock, I replied, 'It's 5.36.'

'What?' she exclaimed. 'Are you winding me up? What are you waking me for at this hour? It's too early. Go back to sleep.'

'I can't,' I whimpered. 'I've got something on my mind. I've been awake all night.'

She sighed in exasperation and clicked on the bedside light. 'What's the problem, then?' she asked impatiently.

'When I was having a drink and watching the football yesterday, I bumped into a friend who told me that he'd seen my brother drinking with a woman in a pub near to the canal.'

There was an unnerving moment of silence that seemed to last for ages but was probably only a few seconds.

Sandy's smile slipped from her pale face. 'Where were you?' she asked.

'I was in the canal-side bar.'

'I thought you were going to stay locally.'

'No, I called a couple of colleagues from work and met them there. We watched the match before Freddy "with a y", a regular in the Bricklayers Arms, came in and told me that he'd seen Kieran with a bird in the Grapes.'

'So what did you do?'

'I went searching in a lot of pubs and bars but I couldn't find them anywhere. I rang his mobile, texted and even called my parents' house but they were out. He didn't respond to any messages or answer his phone. It feels as though something is wrong, very wrong.'

'I wouldn't worry about it,' Sandy said. 'It probably wasn't him. Freddy got the wrong man.' She lay down once more.

'Maybe,' I agreed reluctantly and moved across in an effort to get a cuddle.

To my surprise and disappointment, Sandy recoiled and kicked me hard. 'Stop it.'

'I only want a hug,' I entreated.

'No, I don't fancy it.' She rolled to the edge of the mattress.

'What's the matter?' I asked with deepening concern.

'Nothing. I just don't like being touched. Leave me alone. It's bad timing.'

I eyed her sceptically in the pale light before asking, 'Where did you go, then?'

'Just out,' she snapped.

'Who did you go with?'

'A few friends.'

'Did you have a meal?'

'No, just a drink,' she replied wearily.

'What time did you get back?'

'I'm not sure.' Her tone was becoming increasingly irritated.

'Did you have a good time?' This final inquiry appeared to light the bluetouch paper, on a smouldering firework.

'What's with the cross-examination? Why are you grilling me? What's your problem?' Sandy spat furiously.

'I was only asking because I'm concerned. I care and I worry. I went to bed before you returned and I was asleep and never heard you come in, that's all.'

'Well, stop checking up on me. Stop spying. You should trust me,' she snarled.

'All right, all right,' I said, trying to lower the emotional temperature. But I couldn't stop myself asking, 'So where did you go, what did you do, what time did you arrive home?'

Sandy flung back the bedding, sprang to her feet and flounced towards the door. She cast a withering glance over her shoulder as she bellowed, 'I'm sick of this! I've had enough! It's not working.'

Still in a foul temper, she showered, dressed and left for work. I sat moping, slowly eating a boiled egg and watching through the kitchen window as a yellowish spring sun rose steadily in the east. The unsolved puzzle of her whereabouts and her strange behaviour had unsettled me. I didn't move for more than an hour, trying to make sense of it all.

Finally I decided to contact my brother, not only to find out where he'd been the previous evening but also to outline the get-rich-quick scheme. The ringtone repeated five times before his unmistakable voice gruffly demanded, 'What?'

'Is that you, our kid?' I asked.

'Of course it is. Who did you expect, Father Christmas?' he answered sarcastically. 'What are you ringing for? I am still in the sack and I've not had my breakfast. What's up?'

'Last night I was watching the footie in a boozer in the centre of town and a friend of mine reckoned that he saw you with a girl further along the road.'

There was a moment of hesitation before he asked, 'What's that got to do with me?'

'Were you in Manchester last night?' I enquired.

'Me? No. Why?'

'Like I said, my mate was positive that he spotted you with a brown-haired piece.'

Another brief silence followed. 'It wasn't me. I would have told you if I was coming over. I stayed in last night.'

'So why didn't you answer your phone or reply to my messages or voicemails?' I demanded.

'I left my phone upstairs. The battery was flat so I put it on charge.'

'I rang Mum and Dad's line but it went straight to the answering machine. Why didn't you pick it up?' I persisted.

'I was snoozing in the armchair and couldn't be bothered so I just ignored it,' he explained. 'They're having a weekend away in Bridlington.'

'Oh, yeah,' I grunted begrudgingly, remembering them telling me earlier in the week. 'It just seemed strange that my mate claimed to have seen you. He said that you raised your thumb in recognition.'

'I must have a twin,' Kieran joked. He changed the subject expertly. 'Anyway, how are you?'

'I'm OK. I'm skint, but what's new?'

'Join the club,' he empathised. 'Currently there's no overtime available. These are hard times. I could do with some extra brass.'

'I've been considering an idea for a while that I was going to discuss with you, if you're interested in making some extra dough,' I said tentatively.

'Oh, yeah? What is it?' he asked, a glimmer of interest in his voice.

'I don't want to talk about it over the phone. Why don't we meet somewhere for a drink on Wednesday?'

'No problem; I should be free. What about the Pheasant? It's about equal distance. Around seven o'clock?'

'Fine,' I agreed. 'I'll meet you there. Give me a buzz if there's a change of plan.'

***

Kieran and I met at the agreed time and place. It was a lonely pub that only the hardiest of travellers would find, one of those traditional North Country inns with horse brasses, oak beams, a stone floor and a log fire burning brightly in the corner.

The mutton-chopped landlord poured us a couple of beers and brought them over to our table by the window. 'Aye up, lads. Two of the finest pints around here,' he boasted as he set them down and wiped his damp hands on his pot belly. 'Give me a shout if tha needs owt else. I'll fetch it over cos it's dead in here tonight.' He happily accepted a dodgy note and chugged back to the bar.

For some time we sat in silence. Kieran appeared uncharacteristically withdrawn, I thought, as I surveyed his close-shaven face. Invariably he was dressed scruffily in baggy sweatshirts, dirty jeans and scuffed trainers but today, strangely, he was wearing a freshly ironed shirt, pressed trousers and shoes. Usually, he could not stop talking, but today he was subdued; he was nursing his drink rather than downing it. Something was not quite right; it made me uneasy.

'I still can't shed any light on the supposed sighting of you from last Saturday,' I confessed. 'And on top of that, Sandy's not speaking to me now. We had a massive row.'

'What about?' Kieran asked, juggling with a beer mat.

'She thinks I'm always spying on her, but I'm not.

189

There's a real tension between us and I'm getting worried.'

'So what's your next move?' he asked, flicking the coaster into the air and catching it again.

'I'm not sure. I'm confused. It might be the end of the road,' I said with a heavy heart.

'Never mind, there's plenty more fish in the sea,' my brother said without a shred of empathy. 'Do you want to go outside for a chat now?' he asked, after the landlord brought my change.

We went out into the rapidly fading daylight and plummeting temperatures. We chose a spot furthest from the pub doors, sat on white wrought-iron chairs and I outlined the plot in as much detail as possible.

Kieran asked, 'So you need me to come to the street where the bookies is located, gain access to the external power supply and temporarily disable it on a busy afternoon. Is that about the size of it?'

'Yes,' I confirmed.

For some time he didn't speak as he weighed up the merits of colluding with me. Finally he asked, 'How much is in it for me?'

'Two grand after the job is completed and I've collected,' I offered. I smoothed down the goose bumps on my arms.

He was silent again and his face was inscrutable. Then he stated, 'I'll settle for four.'

This demand for double the original offer rocked me; I considered that the initial fee was very reasonable bearing in mind that his role, although important, was relatively minor. In an effort to reach a compromise, I suggested three.

Reluctantly he agreed, shook hands on the deal and

leaned back with a smile of satisfaction. 'When are you proposing to do it?'

'I'm not sure. It must be soon; we all need the bread,' I replied. 'Probably this Saturday is our best bet because it's the Grand National. The shop will be packed with once-a-year punters who don't know what they're doing. It will be chaos, so if you sort the power cut at exactly 2.30, it will provide a window of opportunity. Sandy can stamp and return my blank ticket while manually processing plenty of others. It becomes less suspicious if my winning accumulator is timed among another dozen or so.'

Kieran said, 'Once I've restored the power, I'll get the hell out of there. There must be no contact between us for a few days afterwards. You can get in touch when you've got the money. If they give you a cheque, wait for it to clear and then draw cash. I want folding stuff only,' he stipulated.

'Got you,' I said before we high-fived, finished our drinks and walked separately to the almost-deserted car park.

I sat in my car for several minutes with the door ajar as my brother drove recklessly away, with headlights blazing, radio blaring and tyres screeching. I began to experience the agony of self-doubt. Was the planning right? Was the timing right? Could we rely on each other? The whole crime hinged on immaculate preparation, perfect plans, split-second timings and everyone playing their part. The consequences of failure did not bear thinking about.

With diminishing enthusiasm, I closed the car door and started the engine. I tried to call Sandy but her number was engaged and remained so as I journeyed home, enveloped by confusion and with distrust spreading like a cancer inside me.

Chapter 22

D-Day

The persistent buzzing of the alarm clock raised me from a fitful and unrefreshing sleep early on the following Saturday morning. The day had come.

Reaching out and swatting the source of the irritation, I contemplated the ramifications of the plan, which was scheduled for later in the afternoon. We could not afford a single mistake; there must be no errors, as I'd pointed out to my collaborators the previous evening. In addition, my brother and I had agreed that we wouldn't contact each other until the dust had settled.

'Are you all right, hon?' Sandy asked, to my astonishment. Throughout the last few days we had barely spoken. She had communicated by banging doors, slamming drawers and breaking crockery.

Perhaps the Snow Queen was thawing, I speculated with a degree of scepticism, before responding guardedly, 'I'm not too bad, thank you.'

'Are we still all set for today? Is the planning spot on?' she asked cautiously as she rolled towards me and propped herself up on her right elbow.

'Yes, I've gone over it countless times. There will be no hitches or glitches,' I answered positively.

She edged closer. 'When we succeed, it will all be thanks to you. You're the mastermind,' she said, attempting flattery.

'Not really. I'm just a cog in the machinery. It's a team effort.'

'That's all very well, but you're the driving force.' She reached across and nuzzled her cheek into my neck.

I was dumbfounded and unprepared for such an obvious gesture of reconciliation. Was this the person who, for the last week, had cooked her own meals, neglected to do the laundry and failed to say goodnight? Could this be the same girl who said that she was sick of it all, did not think it was working and indicated that she wanted to leave?

'You've changed your tune,' I said scornfully, while encircling her wrist like a handcuff to restrain any further movement.

'I know. I'm truly sorry; I was being a silly bitch. When I'm in that type of mood, you should just ignore me and take no notice of what I say. I want this partnership to work,' she said smoothly, with a weak smile.

Like most red-blooded males faced with the scenario of lying in bed with an apologetic, naked goddess who was clearly intent on putting things right, I released my grip, put my arms around her waist and surrendered.

Before Sandy left reluctantly for work, we recapped on the day's project and wished each other good luck as though it were our very last morning together. With the optimism seeping back into my soul, I pottered around the apartment for a couple of hours. However, as the hour of reckoning approached, my mood became more sombre. I sat on the edge of the sofa, mulling over the forthcoming events. Staring intently at my already bitten thumbnails, my fear mounted. I had arrived at a crossroads and I was on the cusp of something that would shape my future.

It is always better to look forward with positivity than dwell on the negativity of the past, I considered, when, twenty minutes later and with my misgivings temporarily suppressed, I left the apartment. Under a lowering sky, I made my way along the unusually deserted road towards the target.

There was no sign of Kieran when I hurried past the isolated black metal electricity box. Although I was marginally ahead of schedule, I experienced a sinking disquiet as I speculated on the possible reasons for his absence. Had he forgotten, got stuck in traffic, or simply got cold feet and changed his mind?

I went into the warm, dry and busy bookmakers. To the left, I observed a gang of shifty-looking workmen in dirty boots chattering excitedly among themselves while huddled around a copy of the daily newspaper. Striving to remain inconspicuous, I slunk to the opposite side of the shop and skulked furtively in an emptier corner. With my head bowed and shoulders hunched, I pretended to study the form guide. However, an old gentleman with stubble and glasses approached me and asked me to help him complete his betting slip. He thanked me profusely for the help, which attracted the unwelcome attention of one of Biffo's buddies who was loitering near the gents.

Shergar galloped across the room and brayed, 'I've got a red-hot tip, dude.'

While the bystanders sniggered, I replied wittily, 'It's probably an enlarged prostate. I'd see a doctor or buy some ointment.'

He smiled, scratched his head in confusion and resumed. 'No, I mean it's a sure thing. Sure as wet weather and as certain as the sun going down.'

Generally his winning selections were as rare as a cabbie without BO, I reflected, before asking, 'Go on then, what is it?'

'Dusty Carpet in the Grand National. The form is solid, the odds are rewarding and it's never been beaten,' he stated.

A few seconds later, and after perusing the list of runners and riders, I failed to identify his choice. I asked, 'Which horse? What number? Who is the jockey?'

'Dusty Carpet; it's never been beaten,' Shergar repeated. He trotted off, wreathed in smiles.

I grabbed a stubby plastic pen and started to chew pensively on the blunt end as the clock ticked down. Checking my watch, I noticed that lift-off time was rapidly approaching as Scottish Marjorie lumbered from the premises on her break. Sandy maintained an expression of pure innocence as she continued to serve a line of punters before winking at me encouragingly. Then, without warning and earlier than discussed, the power supply failed.

In the dim daylight that filtered through the opaque glass door and adjacent windows there was uproar. The regulars behaved like a brood of hens that had seen a fox. In an effort to regain control, a squat manageress waddled into the centre of the shop. Shaking her head and wringing her hands in frustration, she announced, 'Ladies and gentlemen, we seem to be experiencing an outage. I'm sure that it's only a temporary problem and I'm confident that it will be resolved shortly. Meanwhile, if you still have any bets to place, please form an orderly queue and we'll process them manually. Thanks for your patience during this unforeseen period.'

I snatched a blank football coupon from the dispenser and rushed to my co-conspirator's position. Shaking with tension, I was forced to wait behind a dithering old woman who fumbled with her loose change before spilling it randomly on the counter.

After I'd helped her gather up her shrapnel, I eased her aside. Full of trepidation, I pushed the unmarked slip under the protective glass. I seemed to wait forever, while Sandy inspected, stamped and returned it with a nod of approval. Hurriedly, I took the paper and folded it before stuffing it into the inside pocket of my jacket.

I went back to Shergar. 'I'm not bothering with the big race,' I said restlessly. 'There are too many contenders. Anyone who has a bet in that event must have a grudge against their money.'

'Well, let's hope one of us has a profitable day,' he said cheerfully.

The lights flickered on again, the monitors lit up and the slot machines sprang back to life. I left quickly, surveyed the street warily and retreated to the sanctuary of home.

Later I returned to the bookies in time to watch the footie scores appear on the screen mounted above one of the four roulette machines. The scene now was much calmer; the Grand National had been run and the horde of gamblers had dispersed.

At breakfast time I had nominated which ten fixtures to concentrate on and I waited on tenterhooks for the results, before marking the paperwork with a home victory, away win or draw. Thankfully there were no familiar faces among the needy and greedy punters who were still vainly chasing their losses; consequently there were no distractions when the classified results began to scrawl along the bottom of the screen.

I watched hawkishly while completing the form. Finally confirmation of Scunthorpe's success at Accrington Stanley flashed up and I added that as the last leg of my long-odds accumulator. Conveniently, my partner in crime was sitting alone at her position as I handed in the already stamped ticket. She accepted it and concealed it in a stack of unsettled bets.

During the next excruciatingly long half hour, I killed time by feeding £100 of counterfeit currency into an avaricious, fixed-odds betting terminal. As I played blackjack for minimum stakes, I tried valiantly not to watch, wonder and worry.

Immersed in their work and oblivious to me, the staff were preoccupied when Sandy gave the signal. I pressed the cash-out button before removing the printed receipt from the reluctant jaws of the gaming machine and presented it to the cashier for payment. As part of our plan, I handed over both the automated and soccer slips to Scottish Marjorie for verification and settlement.

After counting out the £80 in notes as though drowning her favourite kitten, she frowned deeply, stared disbelievingly and handed the accumulator to the manageress for further inspection. Following an agonising but mercifully short delay, during which there was a lot of whispering, head-shaking and gesturing between the employees, the manageress crooked her finger and beckoned me to the side door.

'Is this yours?' she accused.

'Yes,' I confirmed. 'I believe it's a winner. Every team won,' I confirmed confidently.

'What time did you place the bet?' she asked, still full of doubt.

'Approximately 2.30.'

She scowled, pursed her lips and demanded, 'Was it when the power was off? Because it's got a manual marking and staff initials. I didn't see you in here at that time.'

'I came in just before the power cut. It was busy, noisy and chaotic. Your young assistant with brown hair processed it,' I confirmed steadily and pointed at Sandy.

'This is worth a substantial amount,' proclaimed the boss, brandishing my passport to happiness. 'I must contact HQ to verify it and authorise it. We don't hold much cash on site. Will you accept a cheque instead?'

'No problem. I'll hang on while you phone them.' I didn't flinch or alter my posture, despite a bead of sweat trickling from my forehead, sliding down my nose and dripping off the end.

I waited for a further uncomfortable fifteen minutes before being summoned back to the office, where the woman told me, 'I received clearance to issue your returns in the form of a cheque. To whom shall I make the £47,228 payable?'

'If you just put M Carpenter, that will do nicely,' I

said. Her colleagues watched, totally fascinated. Shaking slightly, I gratefully accepted the game-changing cheque before croaking, 'It's about time I had a good win. It's been ages since I won anything.'

The manageress still looked unconvinced. 'You've had a lucky day then, haven't you? With your success on the machines and good fortune on the footie, I'd hurry along and buy a lottery ticket if I was you, sonny.' She retreated into her office and locked the door.

With my nerves jangling and heart pounding, I fled the scene without looking at anyone. The task had been accomplished successfully.

Chapter 23

Total Devastation

On the following Friday afternoon, I stood in the dappled sunlight on the garage forecourt and whistled tunelessly while filling the tank of my car with petrol. The last few days had dragged inexorably as I waited for the cheque from the bookmakers to complete the clearing process.

Since the previous Saturday, Sandy had not been on duty at the shop and I had deliberately avoided the scene of the crime so we were unaware of any concerns about breaches of security that might have been flagged up by the other members of staff. To my immense relief, I had established via my banking app that payment had cleared without a hitch. I was able to draw against it so, for the first time in my young life, my balance showed a healthy credit of in excess of £50,000.

Boosted by this welcome knowledge, on that Friday I had left euphorically for work as Sandy completed her packing in preparation for her girly weekend on the sun-kissed Spanish Costa. Following some mild persuasion for an extra £500 spending money, she had given me a businesslike farewell before we went our separate ways.

A stout, middle-aged woman with big teeth and thyroid eyes was standing behind the counter when I went in to pay. 'Do you want any of these chocolate bars? They're on special offer today; only one pound each,' she asked.

Rummaging for my debit card, I replied politely, 'No thanks,' and punched in my PIN.

After a short pause, the assistant stated, 'Unfortunately, that transaction has failed. Just try again for me.'

I obliged and put in the numbers again but the same thing happened. Trying to be helpful, she asked, 'Have you got an alternative card that we could try? Or cash?'

'No, I haven't got either,' I started to fidget. 'There's enough in there. I checked first thing so I don't know what the difficulty is. Let me check with online banking.'

I stepped back. With mounting anxiety, I accessed my details. What might have caused this uber-embarrassing situation? Perhaps I'd been hacked or cloned. Maybe there was a malfunction with the software, or the bank was experiencing some technical difficulties. These theories were quickly dispelled when the state of my financial affairs appeared on the screen.

'That's not right. It's impossible,' I complained under my breath as the paltry amount of thirteen pence was displayed.

A wave of panic engulfed me and a bead of perspiration slid down my forehead. Earlier there had been fifty grand; Sandy was taking a monkey so, as I had not used the account, what had happened?

I scrawled frantically up and down the list of transactions. The only one listed for today was a payment of exactly £50,000 to a recipient whose account ended with the four digits 6193.

I glanced up as the now-glowering female broke the silence. 'Have you sorted it?'

'Not yet,' I answered. I stood up. 'There is some kind of discrepancy that I don't understand.' I was starting to panic.

'Well, you still need to pay for the fuel. I've noted your registration. If you provide me with a contact address, we'll send an invoice.' She seemed to appreciate my predicament and was showing a degree of sympathy.

Fleetingly I toyed with the wad of fake twenties that was burning a hole in my trouser pocket but I couldn't do it. There was a risk that she had a note scanner to check for counterfeits stashed somewhere behind the counter. I gave her my details and she urged me to, 'Have a nice day.'

Following my hasty departure from the garage, I parked down a quiet side street and telephoned the bank's customer service team. Fearing disconnection at any moment because of the call handler's inability to grasp the fundamentals of my problem, I spoke to an uncommunicative and uninterested assistant named James. After placing me on hold for twenty minutes, he returned at last and confirmed that a cheque for £47,228 had cleared into my account, my salary had been credited and a withdrawal for precisely £50,000 had been actioned.

I argued lengthily that I'd not given permission for such a large transaction but instead of trying to tackle the matter, he tried to sell me a short-term loan at an extortionate interest rate; he said that would cover the temporary deficit. With my temper nearing boiling point because of his ineptitude and insensitivity, I rudely declined his offer. Unable or unwilling to help any further, James suggested that I visit the nearest branch of the bank and aired my concerns face to face. Reaching the end of my tether, I terminated the conversation then I turned the car round and sped to my local branch.

Rushing into the bank, I marched purposefully to the help desk, where peppermint-sucking, stern-faced Margaret was busily filling in a form. Lifting her gaze and putting down her pen, she asked in a weary voice, 'Can I help you?'

'Yes,' I replied, a little breathlessly. 'I don't know if you remember... I came in a month ago and you helped me with some documentation. Evidently there's been an error on my account. A lot of money has been taken out.'

'I see,' she responded slowly. After a slight deliberation she ordered, 'Sit down and we'll get to the bottom of it.'

I obeyed and, babbling like a brook, began to pour out the whole sorry saga. She remained silent and expressionless. Finally, she pulled the computer keyboard towards her before efficiently retrieving my records which enabled her to view all of my transaction but, in particular, the rogue entry.

'Mr Carpenter,' she began, 'there are no visible issues on your file. Everything seems in order and there are no obvious illegal activities. I can see that a substantial cheque was paid in on Monday, which has now cleared. You received an overnight credit, which I assume are your wages, and an authorised payment left at 8.32.'

'What do you mean? I've not made a transfer. Who's

provided authority?' I demanded angrily.

She said, without diverting her eyes from the monitor, 'There are two authorised signatories on the mandate. One is you and the second is a Miss Gibson. Are those details accurate?' She raised her bushy eyebrows. 'I recall setting up this facility for you. This substantial transaction was made online and the funds were credited to a Sandra Louise Gibson. Is that the same person?'

For several moments I sat like a Trappist monk as the staggering hammer blow started to take its effect. Realisation finally dawned until, pathetically, I whimpered, 'But she was only supposed to take £500.'

'Well, it looks as though she's taken more than you anticipated,' Margaret stated harshly.

'That's fraud, then. Deception! Theft!' I complained loudly.

Margaret merely tugged at her sleeve, shook her head and peered over the top of her spectacles before saying firmly, 'It's not. You added her to the account of your own volition. She has exactly the same rights and access as you.'

'You must reverse the transaction. Recall it! Invalidate it!' I begged.

'No. Why should we? There is nothing untoward and a crime has not been committed. I suggest you contact your partner and sort out the problem. Given your personal circumstances, I did counsel against your wishes but, sadly, you wouldn't listen or respect the advice.' She sounded incredibly smug.

Reluctantly realising that nothing could - or would - be done I leapt to my feet before petulantly flyhacking a wastepaper basket and storming furiously from the room.

Reeling from the shock of the bank's refusal to

help and trying to catch my breath, I contemplated my next move. Deciding that Sandy would have arrived at her destination by now, I fumbled in my jeans before extricating my phone with a shaking hand and speed dialling her number. The ringtone remained unanswered for a couple of minutes until I ended the call. I tried again, with the same outcome.

Clutching at a straw, I tried Jessica's number, where the ringtone repeated five times. Finally, and much to my relief, a friendly female voice answered.

'Is that you, Jessica?' I asked.

'Yes, who's that?' she responded with a slight hesitation.

'It's Mike Carpenter, Sandy's friend,' I revealed.

'Oh hi. How are you? I've not seen you since the quiz night. How are things?'

'I'm OK, thanks. Is Sandy with you?' I asked.

'No, why?' she replied with mild surprise.

'I can't get in touch and I need to speak to her urgently,' I responded. The grim hand of uncertainty tightened its grip. 'Are you in Benidorm?' I enquired.

'Benidorm?' she repeated. 'What do you mean?'

'Isn't this the weekend of the girls' trip to Spain that you were organising?'

There was a long silence. Then Jessica said, 'We did consider it but no one could afford to go, so we shelved the project.'

'That's very odd,' I was finding it difficult to speak and took a deep breath. 'When I left for work, Sandy was packing her bags. She asked for some extra spending money. She told me that she was flying out of the country at noon.'

'Well, she's not with me. I haven't spoken, texted or

heard from her for days. I was going to catch up tomorrow.'

'Haven't you been revising together for the law exams?'

Jessica's confusion was clear. 'I have, but Sandy isn't reading law. She's doing media studies. I thought you knew that.'

'No. I was under the impression she was on the same course as you.'

'No, we just shared a flat, that's all. We're studying completely different subjects.'

I was dumbfounded. I blurted out, 'So you've not gone with her?'

'Obviously not. As far as I am aware, no one has gone on holiday,' she said.

'OK. Leave it with me. I'll try to track her down.' I ended the conversation abruptly. I was starting to feel nauseous.

Confronted by the eye-watering facts, I drove the short journey home. I made one final and desperate attempt to telephone and text Sandy but there was no reply.

By the time I arrived at my apartment, the pieces of the complex puzzle were fitting agonisingly into place. The dramatic and unexplained mood swings since Easter, the fictitious holiday abroad and the plundering of the joint bank account now made sense.

A sickening feeling of isolation and humiliation devoured me as I realised that she had lied, robbed and dumped me. How blinkered I had been not to see the tell-tale signs; how stupid I had been not to understand her erratic behaviour; how forgiving I had been when she'd refused to explain her nights out when I couldn't contact her. I was the architect of my own downfall.

I slammed the front door shut and stormed tearfully

into the living room.

Folded in half and resting on the middle cushion of the sofa was a sheet of white paper. With mounting trepidation and trembling fingers, I picked it up and unfolded it.

Mike, by the time you get this note, I will be far away. I'm out of your life and gone forever. Don't try to find me. Our relationship has run its course.

We've enjoyed loads of laughs and some good times but ultimately you are not what I am searching for. I need danger and excitement, not dependability and steadiness. You are too clingy, too stifling.

Three years ago I met someone special in a Leeds nightclub but we lost touch before meeting again last November. We've been seeing each other since February and have decided to elope. We're making a fresh start and nobody can hold us back. You're familiar with my boyfriend because it is your brother, Kieran.

I took the money to help with our plans. I remember telling you that one day I would be rich and this is the first step on the ladder.

I know that all this will cause you a great deal of heartache and I am truly sorry. I needed you as a stepping stone to better things. You will get over it in time. You're young, handsome, one of the good guys.

I hope that you meet someone nice and find happiness.
Sandy

Blinking back the tears, I let the letter slip from my grasp and watched it flutter to the floor. Her crushing confession of betrayal rendered me speechless. The additional disclosure that my elder sibling, my best mate, my own flesh and blood, had stabbed me in the back almost finished me off.

Sobbing uncontrollably, I collapsed onto the sofa and descended into morbid introspection. Not since I watched Jenny Agutter's heart-wrenching cry of *'Daddy, my Daddy,'* in the film *The Railway Children* had I cried so many tears and I went on crying for the next two days.

The next forty-eight hours were ones of physical and mental darkness. The curtains remained drawn to prevent the world seeing my wasted and abandoned state. I didn't answer the phone, although on one occasion I logged onto the computer and prowled the internet in search of any clues as to my existence with Sandy. There was a blank where my name and profile should have been on her Facebook page. I had been deleted and she had meticulously erased all proof that there was any connection between us.

During that pitiful, lost weekend, I wandered vacantly in and out of the rooms. I conducted a forensic search for evidence that Sandy had ever lived with me. There was nothing. Despite that, a part of me was still hanging onto hope, as a drowning sailor clutches to driftwood. How could this seemingly innocent young woman, who gave herself unconditionally, perpetrate such an evil act? This girl who had captured my heart and taken over my world? This goddess, whom I had really loved, had manipulated me into defrauding her employer, acquiring counterfeit cash and laundering the money. She had convinced me to mastermind the fraudulent betting operation and take the risks; no doubt, in time, I would also carry the can for it.

The mystery of my brother's sighting with an attractive female in a city centre pub was solved. So was his unusually smart appearance and inflated air of self-confidence, his reluctance to answer calls, return messages and reveal his whereabouts.

Searching forlornly in the cupboard, I saw that Sandy's boots, coats and jackets had vanished. Her potions and powders had disappeared from the bathroom. The dresses, skirts and tops had gone from the wardrobe. There was no trace of her existence. Despite the familiar aroma of her perfume, which lingered mockingly in the bedroom, and the paperback lying open and bookmarked by a hairgrip next to the bed, everything had reverted to the state it was before she moved in.

Instead of hearing her infectious laughter, seeing her angelic smile and experiencing her gentle touch at night, I could anticipate days of self-loathing. There would be countless weeks without hugs. Ironically – or cruelly – she had returned faithful old Cecil, with his missing eye, torn ear and patchy fur, from exile. Once again, he crouched shabbily on my pillow.

As Sunday was drawing to a close and I sprawled on the sofa, still weeping, I heard the heavy knock on the front door. Weakened by a lack of sleep, and still despising myself for succumbing to the wiles of a scheming vixen, I rose wearily and shuffled uneasily towards the source of the noise.

Opening the door, I looked out in fascinated horror. Staring back at me were a brace of bobbies, standing like two pints of milk on the doorstep, one full fat and the other semi-skimmed. The shorter officer was a round little man with glasses and hair enhanced by hair gel; the taller one was a beanpole with a waxed moustache and too much aftershave.

'Mr Carpenter?' enquired the porker, with an air of

authority.

'Yes,' I confirmed croakily.

'Mr Michael Carpenter?' he pressed.

'Yes,' I repeated.

'I'm Sergeant Crompton and this is PC Manning,' he stated and flipped open his warrant card. Bleary-eyed, I viewed his credentials. 'We would like you to accompany us to the station to help with our enquiries into a possible fraud and deception committed last Saturday against the local betting shop.'

He reached for a pair of handcuffs.